NELL AND THE RUNAWAY DUKE

SOFIE DARLING

OLIVERHEBERBOOKS

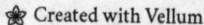

MATLOCK BATH, ENGLAND

11 JULY, 1832

"Even a nob's carriage has an uppity roll to it, you know?"

As Nell stood beside Tilly on the front drive of the Old Bath Hotel and watched said carriage roll down the high street, a dry laugh escaped her. Leave it to Tilly to sum it up perfectly.

Tilly wasn't finished. "Even their horses have their noses in the air, all hoity-toity like." Her assessing eye fell on Nell. "And how long until your next client arrives?"

"Three days," said Nell.

For a year now, two of her most valued clients from the north had been asking Nell to journey up from London and bring the services of *Galante Dressmakers: Extraordinaire* here. As it was summer, she'd finally agreed. The shiny black coach-and-four that had just disappeared around a bend in the road was the first client finished. As Matlock Bath was too far from

London to return between clients, she had three days to herself.

It was a strange feeling.

In Nell's whole life, she'd never once had a holiday. She was a Cockney girl from the East End. Her people didn't holiday. They worked. In fact, they worked so others could holiday.

Tilly waggled her eyebrows suggestively. "That gives us time to see what all Matlock Bath has to offer a pair of chits on their own."

Tilly had been playing dressmaker's apprentice to Nell these last four days, and was clearly aching for a bit of freedom as her gaze cast about.

For her part, Nell simply took in the view. The grand Old Bath Hotel was situated along the inner curve of a bend in the river Derwent, and a lovely green meadow lay between hotel and river, offering a view of the nature surrounding them. Nell hadn't imagined such a place truly existed.

"Now for the people we'll be meetin'," said Tilly.

Nell inwardly groaned. By "people," Tilly meant "gents."

"Will you be givin' them your true identity?"

"I don't see why not," said Nell. In truth, she had no intention of meeting any "people."

Tilly shrugged. "But why not play with it?"

Before becoming a lady's maid, Tilly had met her future employer, Isabel Galante, while working at an exclusive London brothel. Which was to say Tilly was comfortable with switching identities as a situation called for it. Nell, on the other hand, had never been anyone other than Nell Tait.

"What about that Frenchie accent you were puttin' on for a while?" asked Tilly. "You could give it another go."

2

Nell shook her head, adamant on this point. "That's better left in the past."

Her one attempt to be someone other than herself had ended in miserable failure. It wasn't enough to put on a French accent. One had to know a few words, too. Which she hadn't, and the ladies she serviced with her dressmaking skills did… An experiment best forgotten.

Instead, these last several months, she'd been picking up books from a lending library and practicing her pronunciation at night in front of her dressing table mirror. It seemed to be going well. She'd even stopped dropping her aitches, which was an accomplishment in itself. She would never sound like a nob— why would she want to, anyway?—but she could sound like the businesswoman her employers, the Galante sisters, had taught her to be.

"Well, methinks you could loosen your corset a wee bit and let yourself have three days of fun. Our five shillings is paid up for the week," finished Tilly, as if that settled it. "Surely, you can approve of that?"

Nell wasn't sure she could. At least, not the sort of fun Tilly wanted.

Gents… men.

With her bright blonde curls and voluptuous figure, Tilly attracted men like bees to honey.

Nell had absolutely no interest in or intention of attracting men. Men only got a woman into trouble. At least, that had been her experience.

She touched her silver locket, as she always did when she thought about the trouble she'd found herself in at the age of sixteen. *Ewan.* His name, though he'd never drawn a single breath. All she had left of him was the curl of fine red hair that she'd snipped off before they'd pulled him from her. It had taken her two full years of saving to buy the locket. But it had been worth every shilling, for now she was able to carry him everywhere, not only in her heart.

She cleared the familiar ache of grief from her throat. "I have a few notes to jot down regarding Lady Somerton's court dress before I forget." She hoped that would be excuse enough for Tilly. If not, an outright *no* wasn't outside the realm of possibility. After all, she was a Cockney girl born and bred. She could be blunt when the situation warranted, but usually her smile sufficed, for Nell understood the power of her smile.

It wasn't a brilliant smile meant to dazzle. It was smaller and softer. Within her subtle smile was the power to reassure. Sometimes it was reassurance for another. Sometimes it was for herself. And sometimes —oftentimes—it was both. It wasn't a false smile, but it could be a smile borne of bravado. Well, one needed a dash of bravado to go out into the world and do what it took to live within it.

"Face the world with a smile on yer mouth," Mum had always said. *"Even when it kicks you in the teeth. 'Specially then."*

Nell lived by those words every day of her life.

And they served her well.

Thankfully, Tilly allowed herself to be put off. "There's a sweet shop up into the village a little ways. Catch me up when you've finished."

Nell gave a noncommittal nod, which was enough to send Tilly flouncing off with the sort of smile on her face that said she was ready for whatever fun life had on offer today.

Relief speared through Nell, even though she wasn't sure how she could continue to forestall Tilly for the next three days. Her friend was decidedly determined to have a lark, and Nell had no doubt Tilly would find it. For Nell, fun came in different forms, none of them being that of a man.

However, instead of returning to the hotel chamber she shared with Tilly to jot down a few notes as she'd said she would, she found herself crossing the hotel's front drive and stepping onto the green meadow between it and the river. As she took to the gravel path that wound through overgrown shrubberies, the sun shone down on her bright and warm for the first time since her arrival four days ago. It had been raining buckets for days. Truly, where was the harm in taking a little stroll and soaking in the sunshine? She'd never breathed air so fresh.

A lightness entered her step, and a smile lifted about her mouth at the sound of the river rushing in the not-too-far distance. She rounded a bend in the path and the view opened, stopping the breath in her chest.

Across the river towered a broad horizontal slab of limestone, too massive to be believed by anything other than one's own eyes, in some places stark and bare of vegetation, and in others luxuriant in it, as rugged and imposing a sight as one was ever likely to experience. With the river rushing across rock fragments tumbled down from those ancient heights, all one could see and hear was Nature at its most magnificent.

A word hovered just at the edge of memory. One she'd heard a client utter at the sight of a ball gown. "*Sublime*," fell from her mouth. Fearsome, yet beautiful —that was this place.

It wasn't the mannered beauty of the parks in London she'd visited from time to time on her afternoons off. Neither Hyde nor St. James's parks hinted that there could be nature like *this*—wild and rugged and utterly untamed. Nay, not merely untamed, but un-tame*able*. Mankind could never shape a place like this to its fancy, and she loved it all the more for that very quality.

This had been here the whole time she'd been in her hotel room?

This… here… This was her sort of fun.

She pivoted toward the town and thought perhaps a nice amble up the high street might offer a bit of delight, after all.

What harm could come of it?

None she could've predicted, it turned out.

———————————

BELOW A BLUEBIRD SKY, LUCAS RODE INTO MATLOCK Bath astride his favorite Cleveland Bay mare, Lady Mischief, and let the summer sun pour into him. Aristocrats flocked to this popular little spa village in droves to take its curative waters, for both soaking and drinking, which had naught to do with Lucas's purpose today. He was simply passing through as he rode north to discuss leases and farming with Baron Hatton.

At least, that was the official reason for his visit. In truth, Lucas was humoring his mother, for the baron had a daughter of marriageable age, and Mama was most insistent that Lucas meet her.

"A country girl is what you want in a wife, correct?" she'd asked, not precisely upset at the idea, but possibly annoyed by it. "We don't want another engagement broken, do we?"

She was correct on both counts.

He enjoyed the day-to-day running of his many estates and would much rather spend his time in the countryside than in Town, and he needed a wife who felt wholly the same.

Further, it was, indeed, time for him to marry. Not by his age—which was all of eight-and-twenty years—but because of a feeling inside him. He desired the comfort and companionship of wife and family. But she must be the right sort of wife, which was proving difficult. Mama and his sisters, Elizabeth and Catherine, weren't strict society sticklers and had the best of intentions—for the most part—but they loved Town and city life, and introduced him to ladies who only saw his title—*Duke of Amherst*. He couldn't spend his life with that sort of wife. She would be miserable, and he would be, too.

Hence the broken engagement. Lucas still felt terrible about it, but Lady Dorothea's papa had been cheered considerably by all the blunt Lucas had thrown his way to enhance his daughter's dowry for the next match. Lady Dorothea embodied all the qualities of a marriageable young lady—a pretty face and figure; pleasing docility; and thanks to Lucas, one of the largest dowries in England.

But for Lucas, those qualities weren't enough. The woman Lucas was to spend the rest of his life with must see *him*—the man.

He took in the dozy little village of Matlock Bath as he entered on the high street, which was so riddled with mud puddles from all the rain this last fortnight that Lady Mischief had to play hopscotch to successfully navigate the road. With its many shops and hotels catering to the tourists who came for the waters, it put one in mind of a seaside resort town without the sea. Though the natural beauty of the place more than compensated for its lack of ocean, with its river and massive cliffs to the other side. In her novel *Frankenstein*, Mary Shelley had called the area 'Little Switzerland.'

Lucas only realized he'd been daydreaming when a small woman caught his eye. Slight of form and wearing a plain, forest-green pelisse and ivory cotton day dress that wouldn't necessarily differentiate her from half a dozen other young ladies on the street, something about her made it so he couldn't easily pull his attention away. Perhaps it was her faraway gaze and subtle smile meant for no one in particular—or perhaps it was for the ice she was eating. She appeared a bit daydreamy herself.

Lucas only just realized she was poised to cross the street, one foot already in the air for the step down. As he pulled the reins to angle his horse's next step away from her, he miscalculated, and a few happenings occurred at once, the most unlucky being that Lady Mischief planted her right front hoof into a deep black puddle.

As if time had the ability to slow and stretch, a great muddy wave sloshed into the air, arcing higher than seemed possible given the limitations of gravity, and washed over the woman, coating her from head to toe in a wet mess of brown grime.

The woman froze in stunned shock, her ice falling from her hand in an unnoticed splat. In a work of fiction, it would be the stuff of comedy. But here, on the street, it was a decided tragedy.

Meanwhile, Lady Mischief kept tossing her head and letting her displeasure with the situation be known. Lucas stroked her mane and leaned forward to give her a soothing shush. He met the woman's gaze. She remained utterly frozen, except her eyebrows had drawn together. Clearly, what had happened to her was beginning to sink in. Any second now, she would give him the tongue lashing he so richly deserved.

He braced himself for it when her mouth opened and she... *laughed.*

Not a laugh of disbelief or bemusement or even a great expulsion of fury, but a hearty chuckle that sprang from the pit of her belly. So infectious was her laugh that he was almost tempted to join in with her. Then Lady Mischief lifted her front right hoof and tossed her head again. Something was wrong.

He quickly dismounted and grabbed her fetlock. She'd lost a shoe. In the kerfuffle, her back hoof must've knocked her front shoe off in the mud.

Blast.

Now he was stuck in Matlock Bath for the rest of the day, and likely night, while Lady Mischief was reshod. He shook his head in bemusement and flicked a glance toward the woman, perhaps to commiserate in their separate, but linked, misfortunes.

But the patch of cobblestones where she'd stood only moments ago was now empty. She'd vanished.

A pang stole through him. Not of loss—for not even a single word had been exchanged between them—but of something else... of what could have been? Or was it a sense of connection provoked by their shared moment of misfortune?

The fact was she interested him. He didn't know the woman from Eve, but he thought he might already like her. At the very least, he owed her an apology and some coin, too, for her ruined dress and pelisse.

But truly, what woman laughed after getting soaked by a great wallop of mud?

No woman he knew.

He found it intriguing and strangely refreshing.

Now...

Who was she?

NEXT DAY

H er step quiet and unsure, Nell made her way down the dimly-lit, narrow corridor, clutching the bathing dress and cap she'd borrowed from Tilly to her chest, and wondered just what the blazes she was doing here.

Actually, she knew.

And it had everything to do with The Mud Incident from yesterday.

"Lawks, you would think this was London!" Tilly had exclaimed at the sight of Nell, thoroughly outraged on her behalf.

Still reeling in disbelief, Nell had remained sanguine about it all through the bath Tilly had ordered for her in their room. Yet she hadn't been able to get the face of the man who had caused the debacle out of her mind. A handsome face, but one expressing the same reaction as she—particularly when she'd laughed.

Sometimes life delivered mud directly into one's face. It was how one handled the awfulness that mattered, and there were only a few options: laugh, cry, or get angry. The latter two weren't for her. So, she'd laughed and taken herself off to her room and got a good, long look at herself in the mirror.

A complete bedraggled mess of a woman had stared back at her.

And her dress?

It was unsalvageable.

And the man who had been the cause of it?

He'd ridden off unsullied.

Wasn't that just the way of it?

Men.

The foul mood that had swept in refused to budge even after she'd bathed... even after she'd worked the rest of the day into the night... even after seven hours of bed-tossed sleep... even after her morning tea...

"You're as grouchy as Sue Fawn from Pizzy's Pleasure Palace when that hair tincture she got off a barber turned her fine curls to frizz, then made it drop right off her head," Tilly had said first thing this morning. "You never saw such a shiny bald patch on neither man nor woman."

As Nell had never come across Sue Fawn in all her life, she'd have to take Tilly's word. But there was no denying it: She felt decidedly grumpy.

"Right," continued Tilly, "it's off to the baths with you."

"Pardon?" Nell had—by dire necessity—had a bath yesterday.

"We're in a spa town, ain't we? So, go take some of that magic water and cure your mood."

After a few minutes of back and forth with Tilly, Nell had finally conceded the argument and accepted that she would have to take the waters.

Now, she'd paid the attendant her sixpence and was on her way. But as she ventured down the corridor, she noticed two doors at the end, neither marked. Presumably, she was to enter one. She glanced back toward the attendant, who was currently occupied attempting to get into the good graces of a serving girl whose flirty little smile suggested she might be open to the possibility. Nell would get no help there.

Perhaps one was an entry door and the other an exit. What was the worst that could happen? That she would go in through the wrong door?

She chose the one to her right and stepped inside. Instantly, she was assaulted with air that was several degrees warmer than the corridor and sticky with humidity. She did a quick scan of her surroundings and—thankfully—found no one else. She would much prefer to endure this entire experience with no witnesses.

Once she'd found a discreet corner partially obscured by a painted screen, she changed into the bathing dress and cap, her hair tucked firmly beneath. Her first steps beyond the screen were uncertain and unsteady, her feet still clad in sturdy brown boots, though she was fairly sure she was meant to remove them. She felt silly. She'd never worn such a costume, and her hair had already begun to itch beneath the cap.

Still, she was here, so why not give in and find some jolly in the experience?

A smile tugged at her lips, and in an instant, she felt lighter for it. She wasn't the sort who delighted in grouchiness.

She entered a short, dark corridor and made for the light, following the sound of trickling water. The main bathing chamber must be this way. Strangely, nerves fluttered through her as she stepped into a large square room, the ceiling high, the skylight allowing light to pour inside—reflecting off ivory tiles that covered the floor and halfway up the walls, dancing upon glistening water.

If any remnants of her foul mood had remained, they fell entirely away. For the first time since the idea had been introduced, Nell was glad for her holiday. She couldn't swim, but she might not need to, as the large rectangular pool appeared to be no more than a few feet deep.

Seeking to deposit her belongings on a bench—in the East End one didn't leave one's belongings alone in plain sight if one ever wanted to see them again—Nell searched around until she turned and spotted a long row of benches behind her.

A second later, she startled to a halt, the breath catching in her chest as her gaze locked on an extraordinary sight.

It wasn't the sight of the innocent wooden bench that had her frozen in place and her heart threatening to break free and take its chances up the road.

Before her sat a person... a *man*... and not just any man, but...

Him.

The man responsible for drenching her in mud on the high street, ruining her best pelisse. In fact, she might very well still have a dollop of mud in her ear.

But it wasn't the mere sight of him that had a hot blush firing through her. It was the way he sat, legs sprawled, smile curling the corner of his mouth, utterly at ease, and...

Shirtless.

Only a large towel—*thank heavens*—protected the rest of him from view. But what was on view...

Golden, furred chest, ridged muscles...

Oh, what a view.

"You," somehow escaped her parted lips.

He didn't move a muscle. She would know, because she couldn't seem to tear her gaze from them.

"I take it you've made a wrong turn," he said, confident, possibly arrogant.

How like a man.

Tetchy and irritated, her tongue swiped across suddenly dry lips, readying her mouth to speak words she wouldn't dream of speaking under normal circumstances. "Perhaps it's you who has taken the wrong turn."

She'd never spoken such saucy, antagonistic words to a man in all her life.

But this man—well, he deserved them.

A slow smile widened his firm mouth. "Shall we wait and find out who's right?"

She didn't like the sound of that. The sound of his certainty that he was dead right.

Lawks.

But wasn't he a handsome one with his tousled golden hair only a few shades lighter than the hair on his chest—oh, that she knew such a thing about him— the chiseled bones of his face, and eyes the light, hazy blue of a morning sky just before it went deep with the onset of day.

"About yesterday," he began, serious.

He would try to apologize, she understood that, but she was having trouble focusing on the words spilling from his mouth through the cotton—and possibly mud —clogging her ears. His bare chest was stealing clear thought from her brain.

She had no idea *who* this man was, but she knew *what* he was: a man who used his hands. A laborer of sorts. Those muscles hadn't come from nowhere. They came from work.

Yet, otherwise, this man didn't have the mien or speech of a laborer. Perhaps he was an estate manager.

Her body heated another few degrees beyond what even this hot, humid bathing room could incite. And now he'd stopped talking and was looking at her with his brow lifted, as if he expected a response.

"Um," she began and swallowed. "I need you to cover yourself."

His eyebrows drew together as he looked down at his torso. A slight frown formed about his mouth as if he'd only now realized half of him was quite *bare*. It was...

Funny.

Of a sudden, a laugh bubbled up and escaped her. She simply couldn't help herself.

His gaze met hers, and he looked as if he was about to join her when he stopped and cocked his head.

"What—" she began.

He held up a finger, staying the rest of the question in her mouth.

The smile froze on her face. Then her ears picked it up. A sound... a sound that started faraway and was growing nearer with each fluttery beat of her heart. The sound of talking.

Of *men* talking.

"I think we have our answer," he said.

Indeed, they did. She was in the gentleman's bathing room.

Of a sudden, he grabbed the folded towel at his side and shook it open. Before she could question what in the blazes he was about, he'd flung it out and over her head. The world went gray.

Indignation streaked through her. "Who do you think you are? You simply cannot—"

"Shh," sounded low in her ear.

The next moment, the men's voices began echoing off the bathing room's tiles and water. Nell's heart raced in her throat, and the blood pounded through her veins. What new mess had she gotten herself into?

"Gentlemen," said her captor.

Or was he her savior?

The men must've nodded their greetings for the conversation between them didn't miss a beat. Something about the Reform Act that had recently passed Parliament. Nell only knew it because one of her best clients, Lady Mariana Asquith, was quite incensed about the bar to women voting, as it explicitly defined a voter as a man.

A low voice rumbled in the vicinity of her ear. "Shuffle your feet like you're infirm."

Nell immediately got his idea and thought it might work. So, though she would prefer to hie out of this place as fast as her feet could carry her, she shuffled one excruciatingly slow step at a time until, at long last, a hand—*his* hand—wrapped around her upper arm and tugged her to a stop. She heard the twist of a door handle.

Anticipation had her jumpy beneath the towel. Again, his voice sounded in her ear. "I don't recommend shedding this blanket until you're inside the ladies' bathing room."

"Just point me in the right direction," she said in a hushed whisper.

He chuckled and placed his hands on her shoulders. "Five steps, and you're there."

Nell didn't have to be told twice.

She'd taken two steps when his voice sounded at her back. "Meet me."

She drew up sharp, her haste momentarily forgotten. "Pardon?" she hissed, having no idea if they were alone or not.

"Meet me for tea in the Old Bath Hotel at four o'clock."

That was... unexpected. "Hasn't our business with one another reached a conclusion?" she asked, cool, when she felt anything but.

Business? They had no business together. She didn't

even know the man's name. She did, however, know every contour of his chest.

Oh, where had that thought come from?

From the same place that would likely be dreaming about that chest all night, she reckoned.

"I owe you," he said.

Beneath the blanket that was increasingly closing in on her, Nell frowned. A man had never told her he owed her anything in all her life. Something inside her responded to those words and the plea within them, and inexplicably, she said, "I'll be there."

She crossed the remaining few feet to the ladies' bathing room and shut the door firmly behind her. She pulled the blanket off her head and slumped back, instant regret tracing through her.

Why had she agreed?

Men only got her into trouble—and this man in particular. Except...

He didn't appear to be a rogue.

Of course, she knew from experience, it was the ones who didn't appear to be rogues that one needed to keep the closest eye on.

3

H e should be on the road right now.
     Lucas knew that.

Instead, he sat in the tea room of the Old Bath Hotel, waiting... for *her*.

The day had started so innocently. He'd intended to take Matlock Bath's waters before continuing his interrupted journey on a reshod Lady Mischief. Then he'd seen *her*, and that plan had flown out the window, a new plan forming in an instant.

Well, not precisely a plan.

But an urge.

To see her again.

Maybe this time he'd even learn her name.

He snorted. He was acting like an instantly besotted green youth who had never even kissed a girl. He had, in fact, kissed a few ladies in his time—and done more as any other man of eight-and-twenty years—but he'd never kissed *her*.

Where had that rogue—and rogu*ish*—thought come from?

He had no right to it. Yet he felt compelled to know more of her—including the taste of her lips.

Particularly her bottom lip, with its subtle pout.

He settled back into the armchair's worn velvet and resisted the urge to check his pocket watch yet again. Not three minutes could have passed since the last time he'd consulted it. Then, the watch face had read five minutes shy of four o'clock, which meant no more than a pair of minutes would tick by before she was late.

The truth was, he was anxious—even though his appearance gave no indication of his nerves as he sat with an at-ease demeanor, legs slightly splayed, indifferent expression on his face. To all, he would look like any other gentleman of means intent on taking his afternoon tea.

Would she keep her word?

He wouldn't blame her if she didn't, after what he'd already put her through. Mud in her eye, literally... His bare chest... Bad luck, that.

Or perhaps it was good luck.

He couldn't decide.

She hadn't been able to tear her eyes away from his exposed flesh.

Across the tearoom empty of all but a few sprinkled-about patrons, she appeared. Lucas felt his body relax by a subtle degree. Her gaze landed on him, and her step hitched. It wasn't too late to turn around—that was what her good sense would be telling her.

Again, his muscles tensed. Then she took one step, and another, in his direction, and again he relaxed.

She was small and delicate, this woman. Her hair and eyes a soft, amber brown to match. Neat, not a fold on her dress or a hair on her head out of place. She didn't strike him as particularly fussy, but careful. She was the sort of woman who could be easily overlooked —by design he suspected.

But he'd noticed her, and he wanted to keep looking.

Hers was an understated beauty.

And he knew one additional fact about her: She wasn't a lady. The accent of her speech had revealed as much. Yet the manner with which she comported herself was most graceful and genteel.

At last, she reached his table, and he rose at her approach. As they stood opposite one another, silent, assessing, she shifted, as if unsure how to proceed. He gestured toward the chair beside her. "Please."

Primly, she sat, placing her reticule on her lap, as if ready to bolt at the slightest provocation. She watched him with a direct, questioning gaze while he lowered into his chair. He knew what question lay within her almond-shaped eyes. What precisely were they doing here?

A question he was, as yet, unprepared to answer.

So, he started with a different one. "How do you take your tea?"

Her eyebrows crinkled for a quick instant. He'd surprised her. *Good.* "With cream and—" Her gaze landed on the bowl of sugar. Ah, she had a sweet tooth. "One lump of sugar," she finished.

"Or two, perhaps?" he asked. He wanted to tempt her.

Her mouth twitched. Was that a smile seeking the light? "Two would be even better."

He felt himself smile. How was it that he already liked this woman so much?

He poured for both of them—after all, she was his guest, and he wasn't too fussy about the rules surrounding who should be serving whom—and prepared their tea according to their preferences—cream and one... two sugar lumps for her, and black for him. They each took a few sips, observing each other without appearing to observe each other too closely. Still, curiosity could be held at bay only for so long.

"May I be so bold as to ask your name?" he had to ask.

Carefully, she settled her cup into its saucer. "Miss Elinor Tait," she said, quite proper. "Nell," she added, as if correcting herself.

There was something odd about that. "Pardon?"

"Everyone calls me Nell." She gave a self-conscious laugh.

But he felt, strangely, that it was no laughing matter. It was important to her. "What would you prefer to be called?"

Her gaze startled away from the plate of fluffy scones. Surprise shone there. It occurred to him that no one had ever asked her that question.

"Miss Tait," she said at last.

"It's a pleasure to meet you, Miss Tait."

And this time the twitch about her mouth did turn into a smile. A knowing one. Oh, they'd met—and how! —her smile acknowledged.

"And yours?" she asked.

A mild frisson of panic struck through him. Of course, he would need to tell her his name. He had several—Duke of Amherst, Marquess of Greenwich, Earl of Kingston-upon-Hull, and the list of titles went on. He simply needed to pick one.

"Mr. Lucas Kendall," he found himself saying, "at your service."

The name wasn't exactly a lie.

But it wasn't precisely honest either.

His given name was Lucas, and his surname was Kendall, but *Amherst* would've been the proper way to introduce himself to this woman.

But he couldn't.

The admission of his title would destroy the ease that was growing between them in an instant. Her hard-won smile would fade, and she would begin treating him like a duke.

And he didn't want to be treated like a duke.

Well, not by her.

As matters stood now, she saw him as a man. She would stop the moment she heard the word *duke*.

And here was the thing: She didn't have to know.

They weren't in a London drawing room. They were in Matlock Bath, a dozy, little spa town, for a day or two, and then they would never see each other again. So, really, where was the harm in not telling her?

She lost the battle with her clear craving for the scone and reached for it. Discreetly, Lucas pushed forward a dish of clotted cream, followed by strawberry jam.

Again, that little smile appeared.

He'd pleased her.

He liked that.

He watched in silence while she layered cream and jam onto the scone and took a bite. Her eyes shut for a second of bliss. He wasn't sure he'd ever enjoyed anything as much as this woman enjoying that scone.

He envied the scone. To be tasted by her…

To give her bliss…

He cleared his throat. That was no good direction for his thoughts.

She blinked. Such was her bliss that she'd momentarily forgotten about him. Her head canted, and her eyebrows drew together. "I thought your name would start with *Lord*."

"Oh?" Unease crawled through him. "Why is that?"

"It's the way you talk."

"What about it?"

"*Uppity*," she said with finality, as if that one word explained all.

And perhaps it did.

"Well, that's because I am—" How exactly was he planning on finishing that sentence, anyway?

She waited, her jaw suspended in mid-chew, expectant.

"Because..." he said slowly, his mind racing for an answer. Out of thin air, one came to him. "I'm valet to a duke."

Now he'd done it. He didn't even employ a valet, seeing no need for one as he managed to turn himself out decently well. Hopefully, she wouldn't ask about his duties.

A little frown pulled at the corners of her mouth. "And you have to talk as fancy as all that?"

In for a penny... "My father was his father's valet, so I was raised around such speech."

This answer only confused her further, her crinkled eyebrows said. "The duke allowed your father to marry?"

Oh, how the lies kept stacking up. In for a pound... "Yes."

She resumed chewing her scone. She might be young and quiet and prefer to blend into the background, but he would be stupid to take this woman for a fool. Scone eaten, she patted her mouth. "What's it like working for a duke?" she asked, casual but curious. Yet her voice held a small note. It sounded very similar to distaste.

"Do you harbor a grievance against dukes?"

She shrugged one shoulder. "Not so much. It's just that nobs are so high and mighty, you know? They can't seem to help themselves."

Well, wasn't he receiving an education. "Have you met many nobs?" He'd never used that word in his life.

"As a matter of fact, I have."

"Elucidate," he said, with a firmness that sounded no small bit duke-like.

And judging by the cant of her head and the deepening curiosity in her eyes, Miss Tait had caught it. She was just opening her mouth to possibly call him the liar he was when a voice rang out, "Lawks be, Nell."

Both their gazes swung right to find a young lady standing at the table. Well, she wasn't a lady in the strictest sense, with her broad Cockney accent and dress cut an inch low enough to reveal quite a bit of her generous bosom. He and Miss Tait had been so focused on each other they'd entirely missed her approach.

"Is this your—" he began.

"*Friend*," Miss Tait finished for him, challenge in her eyes.

Right. He'd been about to say maid. That was him put in his place.

"Miss Birdwell," said Miss Tait to her friend, "may I introduce you to Mr. Kendall?"

"Oh, sure," said Miss Birdwell, saucy smile curling up one side of her mouth.

"A pleasure," said Lucas, rising and giving a shallow bow.

Both women stared at him as if he'd sprouted another head. He took it that men in their social circle didn't bow.

"Well," said Miss Birdwell, brow lifted, "ain't you a right fancy one?" Her gaze shifted toward Miss Tait. "Where'd you find him?" She gave him a quick up-and-down assessment that seemed to like what it saw. "And does he have a friend?"

"Oh, it was definitely him who found me yesterday," said Miss Tait.

In an instant, Miss Birdwell's eyes narrowed with accusation. "What are you doin' stridin' about on your big, fancy horse and splashin' women with mud on the street?" she demanded, indignant on her friend's behalf. "You look like you'd have better manners, but that goes to show you can't tell nothin' about a person by lookin' at 'em."

Lucas flicked a glance toward Miss Tait. She simply sat quiet during her friend's dressing down of him. He realized two things.

She agreed with her friend.

And he deserved it.

He liked the woman sitting across from him, but she might not like him.

He was determined to remedy that situation. "Miss Tait," he began, refusing to release her gaze. He wanted her to see his earnestness. "I offer my most sincere apology for the events of yesterday. I am entirely at fault and would like nothing more than to replace any items that were damaged."

Miss Birdwell snorted. "Can't replace a woman's pride that easy."

Lucas continued holding Miss Tait's gaze. It was *her* forgiveness he was seeking. "And for the events of this morning," he added.

"What's this?" asked Miss Birdwell, alert. "Nell, you ain't told me—"

"Tilly," said Miss Tait, firmly, "I'll meet you in our room at the half hour."

Reluctantly, Miss Birdwell nodded her acceptance, but she was clearly none too pleased about it. As she walked away, Lucas discreetly consulted his pocket watch. He had fewer than fifteen minutes left with Miss Tait. For a reason he couldn't rightly fathom, he wanted more minutes than that.

Miss Tait held him within her unflinching gaze. She looked to be measuring the weight of his apology. He'd meant it with every ounce of his being. He hoped she felt that. At last, she said, "I accept your apology, Mr. Kendall."

Relief coursed through him. "You're too gracious."

"Tell me, how is your horse?"

"Oh, Lady Mischief, she's—" He stopped right there.

Perfectly well, he didn't say. She was reshod and ready to ride at his command.

Except *he* wasn't ready.

"She needs further tending," he said. "I'll be here a few days more. And you?"

Please don't say you're leaving on the overnight coach.

"A few days yet for me, as well. My clients don't arrive until the fifteenth."

"Clients?" he asked to buy time and information. The fifteenth... Today was the twelfth.

"I'm a dressmaker in London."

"Oh?" he asked. A simple calculation told him that left Miss Tait with a few free days.

"Indeed. We all have a living to make, don't we, Mr. Kendall? Speaking of which, won't the duke expect you back?"

"I've sent word that I've become delayed."

A smile curled her mouth. He'd amused her, unwittingly.

"What is it?" he asked. He wanted nothing more than to know, so he could amuse her again.

"I reckon the duke will just have to dress himself."

"I reckon he will."

They smiled at each other as if they'd formed a conspiracy together.

"What will you do with yourself until the fifteenth?" he found himself asking.

She gave her head a bemused shake. "Plenty of sewing for the last client between now and then."

Lucas didn't like the sound of that. "You're in a spa town. Why not take part in the pleasures on offer?" He hadn't intended the question to sound lascivious, but he thought it might.

She didn't seem to notice. "That didn't work out so

27

well this morning." A beat. "I've never had a holiday, and I'm afraid it shows."

"*Never?*" How could that be?

His befuddled response pulled a laugh from her, and she shook her head at him. "You've been living among aristocrats too long."

"How so?"

"You really don't know?"

"Enlighten me."

"My sort—*our* sort—don't *holiday.* But *you* are an exception, because you've been around it most of your life. You travel with the duke, correct?"

"Erm, correct." Only too correct.

She spread her hands as if her point was proven. "There you are. May I give you a spot of advice?"

"As you like."

"Don't ever lose your place with this duke."

"Why is that?"

"Because you wouldn't like the come-down from the lofty heights where you've been flying. Solid earth would give you a right smack on the bottom."

Lucas decided right there. He no longer wanted to spend more time with Miss Tait. He *needed* to. She was unlike any woman he'd ever met. It was her point of view. He liked it. She had a light and lightness to her, and he needed more of it.

"Allow me to show you the sights of Matlock Bath tomorrow, Miss Tait," he said. Was that desperation in his voice?

She started slightly, clearly taken aback by his boldness. "Why would you want to do that?"

He couldn't very well say the truth, that it was to spend more time with her. So he could know her better. Such words would be too direct, too honest. They would frighten her off, for it was too easy to see the skittishness in her eyes.

"By way of apology," he said, only thinking of the words as they passed his lips. "I am responsible for ruining your frock, after all."

"And my pelisse," she added. The smile hadn't left her soft amber eyes even as they considered his offer.

On tenterhooks, he waited.

Her fingertips gave a few taps on the table, then stopped. "It could be fun."

Did those four words mean what he thought they could? "Is that a yes?"

"Yes."

He allowed no space between her assent and his next question. "How about morning?" He wouldn't give her time to change her mind and beg off. "Ten o'clock?"

She shook her head. "I'll need the morning to myself, so I can begin stitching a few items before my next client arrives. After noon would be best for me."

"One-of-the-clock, then?" How desperate could he possibly sound?

Her head tipped to the other side, and a question entered her eyes.

"What is it?" he asked, bracing himself.

"Why is it you want to spend time with mousy little me?"

The question emerged light and without a hint of self-consciousness.

Fortunately, the answer was easy.

"I don't see you that way."

They were the truest words he'd spoken all day.

A light blush pinked her cheeks. She'd heard that truth.

When she rose to take her leave, he stood, too. Like a gentleman. Well, it couldn't be helped. Some manners were so deeply ingrained they'd become part of him.

"I'll see you on the morrow," she said, and pivoted.

Lucas resumed his seat and watched her navigate a

path between empty tables and chairs as she made her way out of the tea room, graceful and delicate as a bird, her hips a gentle sway beneath her skirts, enough to reveal a hint of the curves underneath.

He couldn't quite understand himself. He'd just told a passel of lies to get a woman to spend an afternoon with him, when all he'd needed to do was apologize and compensate her for frock and pelisse. He simply hadn't been able to end their acquaintance with such finality. When he was around her, he had no desire to be anywhere else.

Perhaps in getting to know her more fully he could better understand this need in himself. That way, when they inevitably parted in a few days, he would've exhausted the feeling by letting it run its course.

And perhaps that feeling wasn't on his side only, for he'd detected a spark of interest in her eyes.

Perhaps she, too, wanted to know more of him.

It seemed too much to hope for.

And yet, he did.

4

Nell and Tilly stood before the mirror, heads tilted in study, staring at Nell's reflection. At last, Tilly said, "That'll do right nice."

Tilly might be a lass with a bit of cheek and an eye for flash, but she told the truth. Also, she was quite a skilled lady's maid, who could do wonders with hair. Nell looked... Well, she looked better than possibly she'd ever looked, wearing her finest mint-green dress and matching pelisse, her hair styled by Tilly.

"Now, about them valets," Tilly said, warming to her role of wise, older friend, never mind they were of an age. "You got to watch out for all men, but valets in particular. They can be right cheeky. It's from hangin' about lords all day. And the handsome ones?" She gave a rueful smile that spoke of a particular weakness in herself. "That Mr. Kendall does make the blood run a mite hotter, don't he?"

Nell gave herself one last look in the mirror and grabbed her reticule off the dressing table. "I can manage Mr. Kendall."

A noncommittal, "Hmm," was all Tilly spoke in response.

Oh, why had Nell agreed to a day out with that man?

Actually, she knew why. Yesterday, she'd been all set to go back on her agreement by telling him the truth: It would be best if they never saw each other again.

Then he'd spoken the words that made it impossible.

I don't see you that way.

No one had ever said anything like that to her, and his words touched on a possibility. Perhaps he didn't see her as a little mouse, her childhood nickname. Which meant he saw her as... *what?*

She didn't rightly know, but against all good reason she wanted to find out.

"Now, that's not to say you shouldn't go," said Tilly after a moment's reflection. "A woman can stand to get into a bit of holiday trouble with a strappin' man like Mr. Kendall. He has nice eyes."

Mr. Kendall did have nice eyes. But his eyes weren't the problem. Simply put, Nell had no experience with a "bit" of trouble. The only man she'd ever had dealings with had gotten her into the big sort.

She touched her locket. *Trouble* was what everyone called it, but that wasn't how she remembered the product of that trouble.

Soft... precious... the very essence of sweetness... Ewan.

A thought she had every day of her life, sometimes more than once. But instead of grief, it brought her comfort. It made her days worthwhile. Her life lived was for the both of them.

She took her leave of Tilly, who gave her a parting wink and a giggle. A trepidatious smile on her mouth, Nell made her way down the corridor and through the Old Bath Hotel. Already decided she would wait no longer than three minutes, the instant she stepped inside the reception room, she saw she didn't have to wait at all. There, across the worn parquet floor and threadbare Aubusson carpet, Mr. Kendall stood with an idle shoulder propped against a wall, his gaze having registered her appearance.

Lawks, but he was handsome with his dark blond hair and hazy blue eyes, not to mention tall and broad-shouldered. Every female eye in the room cut discreet glances his direction—some not so discreet. But he wasn't waiting for any of those women. He was waiting for *her*.

And she'd be a liar if she said it didn't give her a thrill.

He pushed off the wall and closed the distance between them. He smelled nice, too. *Sandalwood.* She reckoned a valet would smell good, proper grooming being part of his job and all. "Did you enjoy a pleasant evening?" he asked.

"Aye, I did," she replied, the words a calm lie. Actually, she'd been as buzzy as a bee in spring. All she'd been able to think about was this very moment—seeing him again.

"And your morning?"

"Productive." Actually, she'd dared not attempt to poke needle into fabric. She'd been so jittery with nerves she was afraid of ruining the fine dupioni silk gown with dropped stitches.

"Do you enjoy your work?" he asked.

Nell got the feeling he wasn't merely being polite, but that he was genuinely interested in her answers. She wasn't sure what to make of it. "Mostly," she said, honest.

"What don't you like?"

"My eyes." Again with the honesty.

His eyebrows drew together. "Your eyes?"

"They're developing a squint." Realizing he wouldn't

33

know what she meant, she added. "At the fine needlework."

Still, he asked, "What does that mean?"

"Dressmakers only have so many years in their eyes. Mine are going early." At his look of concern, she said, "But I can keep running the shop and taking on more apprentices."

He nodded slowly before glancing down, seeming to find something fascinating on the floor. He met her gaze again. "How are your boots? Are they sturdy?"

"Yes," she said, drawing out the word. She wasn't sure she liked the sound of that question. But before she could properly investigate his reason for asking, he crooked his arm and held it out to her.

She hesitated. It wasn't that she didn't know what to do—she was to weave her arm through his. But the thing was, a man had never offered her his arm. Not even when she'd been sixteen and had a suitor.

Suitor? She wasn't sure he could be called that. There was another word for a man like that, and with this man's arm held out to her, she didn't want to think about *that* man.

The blood inciting a sudden riot in her veins, she threaded her arm through his, at last. Through layers of muslin and wool, the heat of his body met hers, inviting her to snug closer as they made their way outside. Though it was another clear day, cool snapped through the air. An urge insisted she make use of his body warmth. That same urge didn't think this man would mind much, or at all.

But she would mind.

Very much.

So, she didn't.

"May I ask where you're leading me?" It was only responsible to ask.

"How sturdy did you say your walking boots are?"

Nell blinked. "I didn't."

Mr. Kendall smiled. She liked his smile, but she wasn't sure she liked *this* smile. This smile was telling her that he had some mischief in store for her.

Once they'd walked clear of the hotel, he stopped their progress, turned, and pointed. "You see that hill over there?"

"Yes…" The hill—it might be a mountain—was hard to miss.

"It's called Masson Hill, and we're going to climb it."

Nell's right foot caught on her left, but she recovered from the stumble when his arm pulled tight, righting her in an instant. How strong he was. A memory of his bare chest and arms flashed across her mind, making her body heat up by an uncomfortable degree.

And that naked flesh was but a few layers of clothing removed from hers.

She would start perspiring any moment now.

Best to concentrate on the matter at hand and not… bare chests. "You're not serious."

He couldn't be.

"You'll find that I am."

She studied the hill. It was woolly with trees and shrubberies and… entirely too massive to consider climbing.

Before she could voice a sturdier objection than the one she'd already made, he said, "You can do it, Miss Tait."

And there it was again. His belief in her.

Oh, how she liked it.

Too much.

Then, inexplicably, she nodded, and he smiled, and she realized a woman might agree to just about anything to coax a smile from a man like Mr. Kendall.

Oh, she was in trouble.

No doubt about it.

But perhaps it was just the sort of trouble she could afford to get into. After all, she would never see this man again in a few days.

Perhaps Tilly had the right idea.

Perhaps a holiday was all about getting into the right amount of trouble.

———

NOT HALF AN HOUR LATER, NELL WAS REGRETTING her *yes*.

London, where she'd been born and bred, was flat, and this "hill" was decidedly not. It was, in fact, interminably, obstinately *steep*. So steep it had her huffing and puffing at Mr. Kendall's back. So steep she wasn't at all embarrassed that her huffing and puffing was the only sound for a mile around besides the crunch of their footsteps making the ascent in steady, dogged progress.

Really, though. The man had coated her in mud upon their first encounter. Bared his chest in their second. Now this marching her up what she decided was definitely a mountain.

What new torture would he devise next?

Actually, that wasn't quite true.

His bare chest hadn't been a torture on her eyes, at all.

"Almost there," he called over his shoulder. "Are your boots holding up?"

"My boots are the least of my worries," she puffed.

"Would you like a rest?"

"Best if we keep on." She took a few steps before she added, "I might be tempted to turn around if we stop."

The man had the temerity to snort.

A thought only now occurred to her. "Are you familiar with this place?" she asked, unable to keep a note of accusation out of her voice. He was entirely too adept at scaling this large "hill."

"I visited several times as a child. My—the duke's family seat isn't very far south of here."

"Hmm," she grunted.

"Is my pace too aggressive?"

Nell would've thought she had more pride than to say, "Aye." But it turned out she hadn't.

Blessedly, he slowed his step so she could draw abreast of him and catch breath that hitherto had refused to be caught. She flicked him a quick glance. "And this is your idea of a nice holiday?"

"I don't mind it," he said on a shrug. "Besides—"

"Yes?"

"You'll see."

A frustrated grunt sounded through her nose. "The right amount of trouble, my sweet arse," she muttered beneath her breath.

"Pardon?"

She was too winded to feel sheepish. "Oh, sometimes the Cockney in me needs letting out. Don't mind her."

He darted a surprised glance her direction and laughed. "I'll take that as a promising sign that I haven't entirely botched the day by bringing you up here."

"I wouldn't get ahead of myself, if I were you." Even as she spoke the words, she could feel a smile wanting out.

"In my defense," he said, "the hill is considerably steeper than I remember from my youth. It's just that —" He hesitated. "I thought you might enjoy what I want to show you up there."

And like that, Nell's pique fell away. It was impossible to remain irritated with the man when he was being so... sweet.

Even if he was marching her up a mountain.

She wasn't sure she'd perspired so much in all her life.

Soon, the trees and shrubberies fell behind them, leaving only low-lying grasses and exposed rock. They'd topped the hill. "Oh, my," fell from Nell's mouth. She turned and turned and kept turning. "There's no end to this view, is there?"

Below them, the countryside stretched for miles in all directions with its verdant rolling hills, dales, and valleys, a river winding like a lazy snake through the landscape here, and a church steeple straining up to meet the heavens there. A thousand feet below stretched England in miniature.

"This must be how kings and queens feel all the time," she said, wonder in her voice.

"How?"

"Like the world is at their feet."

Mr. Kendall chuckled, the sound a warm, deep rumble in his chest. Nell felt the strongest urge to reach for his hand, which must be resisted. Instead, she stepped farther away from him and pointed toward the river Derwent and the broad mass of stone that had inspired such awe in her only a few days ago.

He moved to stand by her side, but, thankfully, made no offer of his arm. "That is the High Tor. It's over three hundred and fifty feet high."

"Lawks," Nell whispered. "All of *this*"—she gave her arm a wide sweep—"it's all nearly too much, isn't it? Folks in London—in the East End, where I come from —they haven't the foggiest about *this*. If they did..." She wasn't quite sure where her words were leading her.

"They would what?"

She tore her gaze away from the view and looked at Mr. Kendall, a man who, though he was a servant, had never wanted for anything in his privileged life. "They might make a fuss about having a holiday every so often. Because this place—" Again, she swept her arm about in the sort of grand gesture made by others, but never by her. She'd simply never been the sort of person who needed to prove a point. But today, *now*, she was. "It belongs to every English man and woman, doesn't it?" A beat. "Not just the nobs. If a person can get here, they can partake of it."

As Mr. Kendall's gaze remained locked onto hers, she detected agreement, and something else, too. *Appreciation.* It sent a novel feeling soaring through her. This man, whom she hardly knew, listened to her—*saw* her. Few did, or cared to. She was simply Nell—little mouse —to all the world.

Except him.

I don't see you that way.

How seductive those six little words.

"Thank you," she said.

"You don't have to—"

"Yes, I do. Today, you've showed me a world I had no notion of and wouldn't have found on my own, so I thank you."

She and this man had lived very different lives, yet she felt their outlooks weren't so very dissimilar.

"May I show you something else?" he asked.

"Anything," she said.

And, strangely, she meant it.

She'd known this man for fewer than a handful of days, yet there was something about him.

She could trust him.

5

The look in Miss Tait's warm amber eyes sent a feeling stealing straight through Lucas. A novel feeling. One that until this very moment he hadn't known he craved.

To have her trust.

But another feeling slipped in alongside it.

Guilt.

To have her trust wasn't enough.

He must be worthy of it.

And was he?

He'd let her believe a falsehood about himself, and was continuing to. But...

Was it a falsehood that mattered? Didn't his false-hood make it possible for them to be fully themselves with each other? Didn't his falsehood make this moment possible?

For somehow, in lying about who he was, he was able to reveal himself more fully.

It was a topsy-turvy logic, but it held in his mind.

Right.

He crooked his arm for her to take. She only hesitated a heartbeat before she slipped her hand through, and delicate as a bird, set her palm on his forearm. "So," he said, as they began walking, "there's something in-side this hill, or was."

Curiosity lit within her eyes. "Oh?"

"Lead. Up until fifty years ago, this was, in fact, the most important lead-mining area in the world."

"As grand as all that?"

"Below our feet," he continued, sensing her interest, "stretching down hundreds of yards, are miles of lead mines. Well, former lead mines. Now, like the rest of Matlock, they're part of the tourist trade."

"How so?"

Lucas spotted a man a dozen yards away, the one he'd been keeping half an eye out for. "See that man there?"

"Aye."

"He'll be our guide down into one of the larger caverns."

"Down?" Her brow lifted. "Into the earth? Will we be able to walk upright?"

"Certainly."

The glance she cut him held no small amount of skepticism.

Soon, they were exchanging greetings with their guide, Mr. Morris, who handed them each a small lantern in exchange for the agreed-upon ten shillings. Passage was usually one shilling per tourist, but Lucas had arranged for himself and Miss Tait to have the cavern to themselves, which came at a price. Half a guinea, to be exact.

For her part, Miss Tait stood back, head tipped to one side, regarding the dark, gaping mouth of the entry tunnel with a healthy amount of wariness.

"This mine here was known as Nestor's," said Mr. Morris as he ducked his head and led them through the entrance, his voice bouncing off rough stone to all sides, darkness enveloping them.

It wasn't long before they were entirely dependent on the lanterns for light. With the dark came damp, too, moisture weeping down the walls of the narrow passage that was only wide enough to allow Lucas's shoulders through and making the clay beneath their feet slick. Judging by Miss Tait's careful steps, she'd noticed.

Mr. Morris continued, "But we don't call it by that name no more. Great Rutland Cavern, it's now known by. Or Royal Rutland, as nobs journey here from time to time, even foreign ones."

"When did it open to tourists?" asked Miss Tait. Her leeriness, thankfully, was giving way to natural curiosity.

"Near about twenty years ago."

"And how do you know the way so well?"

"Ah, that be an easy one. I were a miner here, weren't I? In me youth. And I'll tell you one thing for free. Showing the likes of you around is a sight easier on the old lungs."

Of a sudden, the passage widened and opened into a massive, cavernous space. Rough and rugged, it held its own sort of hard beauty. "This room is Nestus Grotto, and if you sit right here"—Mr. Morris indicated a flat stretch of rock that could serve as a bench—"you'll be able to see something."

Before Miss Tait could take the proffered seat, Lucas held up a hand to stop her. She watched him quizzically while he removed a handkerchief from his interior coat pocket, shook it open, and spread the linen flat on the stone. "If you please," he said with a flourish.

Miss Tait emitted one of her nervous, little laughs. It was clear to Lucas that she was rarely treated so— with gallantry. No one considered her, and his doing so flummoxed and possibly unsettled her. Still, she took a seat on the protective white square, and he sat beside her, his thigh just brushing hers, provoking a decidedly *un*gallant feeling within him.

"Now," said Mr. Morris, "turn your lanterns down to a flicker, then look straight up."

"What are we searching for?" asked Miss Tait, her head tipped back, gaze already scanning the high ceiling which appeared to be naught more than a deep black void.

"Give it a minute," said Mr. Morris. "Your eyes will get there."

An instant later, Miss Tait gasped. "*Ah.*"

Lucas tore his eyes away from the exposed length of her throat and followed her wide, amazed gaze up. Then he saw it, too. High above their heads, through pitch black, appeared tiny pinpoints of light, dozens of them—perhaps hundreds—like stars in the sky.

"Are my eyes deceiving me?" asked Miss Tait. "Where is the light coming from?"

Mr. Morris laughed. "The sun, of course."

"How is that possible?"

"Well, there be holes in the rock, and on a bright day like the one we got today, the light shines through, don't it. Some folks got a name for what you're looking at. Call it the Devil's face."

Miss Tait shook her head. "It's too marvelous to be the work of the Devil."

"Now, if you'll be excusing me, I'll meet you outside." Mr. Morris tipped his flat cap at Lucas and took himself off. Had the man winked?

Miss Tait didn't notice. "How wondrous is this planet of ours."

Low lantern light flickered golden against her skin, and Lucas hadn't a care for any wonders of the earth, save the one before him—the unexpected, unforeseen wonder of this woman.

How lovely... how delicate she was.

And she was separated from him by mere inches.

How easily he could sidle closer, slip his hand along the nape of her neck, angle his face down, and... kiss her.

None of which he could do, in reality.

He shot to his feet, instead. Safer this way.

He began a close inspection of a rock formation. Or pretended to, all the while attuned to Miss Tait's movements as she drew nearer. It only now occurred to him that she might be curious as to what had so utterly captured his attention.

"What have you found?" he heard at his back.

Blast.

Didn't she understand she was in danger of a thorough kissing?

He was just pivoting to achieve greater distance between them when his worst fear—and truest desire— came to pass. Miss Tait emitted a startled, "Oof!" as her feet slipped out from beneath her on moist clay. Without thought, his hand shot out and grabbed her before she could tumble to the ground. Then she was in his arms, mouth parted, bright eyes fast on his, the length of her lithesome body flush against him, the only sound in the cavern the rapid in and out of their breath—hers from a scare, his from... something else...

Desire.

Then her eyes did it.

They lowered to his mouth.

And her tongue swiped across her pouty lower lip.

And there was nothing else for it.

His head angled down, and his mouth touched hers in what could be called a whisper of a kiss.

If it hadn't gone farther.

A tiny groan escaped Miss Tait, and she lifted to her toes, her arms sliding around his neck, deepening the kiss, her tongue slipping between his lips. *Sweet.* She tasted sweet, as he'd known she would, her floral scent of subtle lavender combining with his of sandalwood. One hand found the small of her back and pressed into the undulous curve, drawing her closer. Though small, she wasn't without feminine curves, his body was quickly discovering... and responding to—the hard length of his manhood making itself known between them...

Which was the snap of reality he needed.

Somehow, he tore himself away from her mouth, taking her shoulders in both hands and setting her apart from him. They stared at each other, panting.

"I shouldn't have done that," he said, not as firmly as he should have.

Her head canted. "Why not?"

He ran a frustrated hand through his hair. "Because you're good and an innocent."

Blast.

She stared at him for three ragged heartbeats too long, then did the impossible.

She laughed.

When she finished, she regarded him with a quizzical expression, as if assessing something about him and finding difficulty reaching a conclusion.

"What is it?" he asked. He wasn't sure he wanted to know.

"Is being an innocent the only way for me to be good in your eyes?"

"Pardon?" He hadn't expected that. He would much prefer a justified slap across the face.

"It seems men think that about women." She shrugged. "I think I'm good." She swallowed. "But I'm no innocent."

"*Pardon?*" He couldn't have heard her correctly.

"And," she continued, firm, definite, "if me being an

innocent is the only way we can be friends, then it's been nice knowing you, Mr. Kendall."

Well, that was certainly him put in his place. Except... Oh, how could he put this... "You don't seem like the sort of woman who goes around, erm, not being innocent."

Again, she laughed, which was a bit of a relief. "It has been a while since I've been *not* innocent. Years, in fact," she added.

Lucas would have discreetly left the subject there, but for one thing. The note of sadness that threaded through the words and hovered about her. "Did a man" —he didn't want to speak the next words, but he must —"harm you?" He couldn't tolerate the idea, but he needed to know.

She eased away from him, as if she needed distance for what she was about to say. Lucas braced himself.

"Like too many girls, I once thought I was in love."

The words were spoken lightly, as mere anecdote. Except they held an ineffable heft that was neither light nor mere.

They were words that had shaped this woman's life.

"But that's not really the beginning," she said. "Ever since I was a little girl, I wanted a family, one of my own."

"That's not too unusual, I would think."

"Except I was the fifth of seven children. You would think I'd had enough of big families. But Mum was a washerwoman, and had ideas about the way her house should be run after Papa died. Tighter than the military, it was."

"How old were you when he died?" Lucas's own father had perished before he could form a memory of the man.

"Four years." Her face transformed with a faraway smile. "I remember his beard. It was soft, and he let me

47

braid it." The affection she still held for her father was clear. "In Mum's house, we were all expected to contribute to the coffers once we were old enough to come by work."

"That seems…" Lucas wasn't sure he could finish the sentence without insulting her.

"*Harsh?*" she said, intuiting his unspoken word.

He nodded.

She smiled. "You would think that."

"What do you mean?"

Now it was she weighing words, afraid of offending him.

"You can say anything to me," he said.

"You would think that," she said, "because you're not versed in the realities of the world."

"Are you saying I'm soft?" Perhaps he was a bit offended.

"Oh, I know of one thing that's hard about you," she said on a laugh.

Lucas thought he might blush. He wasn't accustomed to this side of Miss Tait. Her saucy side.

"But there is a softness in your heart, Mr. Kendall," she clarified. "I like that about you."

She liked something about him.

It was a start.

"When I was fifteen," she continued, "my sister got me work as a scullery in a tea shop." She drew a deep breath. "And that's where I met Tommy Trumble. He was… older."

Lucas could already tell that he wanted to punch this Tommy Trumble directly in the nose.

"Tommy was a pretty talker, told me all the things I wanted to hear, anyway. Somehow, he knew what I really wanted."

"And what was it you really wanted?"

She shrugged, wry and slightly sheepish. "A house in

the country. An arched gate with roses blooming all over it. Garden full of green grass. Half a dozen children. The sort of life that didn't rely on makeshift work to make one end meet the other. Then…"

When Lucas could wait no longer, he said, "Then?"

"Then I turned up with child."

Oh.

"At fifteen?" He was shocked. Truly so.

"I was sixteen by then," she said. "And I told Tommy."

Lucas understood this story didn't end well. "Then?"

"I never saw him again."

There.

Lucas felt as if the bottom had dropped from his stomach. He saw the pain in her eyes, heard it in her voice, and didn't know how to make her feel better, and he wanted to.

"I was a stupid girl."

He wouldn't stand for this. "Trumble promised you a life—one you desperately wanted—and you believed him. That doesn't make you stupid."

"Doesn't it?"

"No. It makes you open to life and love. He took your trust and betrayed it." But her story hadn't reached its conclusion yet, and he wanted to know. "And the child?"

Her jaw clenched, and her eyes grew shiny. "He was born still." She tugged at the delicate silver chain around her neck and pulled a locket from beneath her bodice. "*Ewan.* Born with a head of the brightest red hair you ever saw. I have a lock of it in here." She tapped the locket.

"So you always have him with you."

"It's all of him I have left."

"Except what's in your heart."

She nodded and cleared her throat. "The next

morning, word reached Mum of a babe who needed wet nursing."

"And you agreed?" He wouldn't use the word harsh. But that wouldn't stop him from thinking it.

"I hardly knew what I was doing, truth told, but I went. As I was leaving, Mum told me I didn't ever have to come back. So, I didn't."

"You haven't seen your family since?"

She shook her head. "You have to understand. There were too many of us, and I'd found a new situation—a good one, it turned out."

"But she couldn't have known that."

"You take your luck where you find it in this world, Mr. Kendall, and I don't hold any grudges against Mum. Nursing Ariel was a great comfort to me after I lost Ewan, and his mum and aunt, Eva and Isabel Galante, well, they became my family. And now that they've both married lords, I run their dressmaking shop. I hold no hardness in my heart."

Looking into her soft amber eyes, Lucas believed her. How impressive was this small woman who had described herself as a little mouse. Didn't she know she was a lioness? Every obstacle thrown at her she'd turned into a success. "I've never met anyone like you, Miss Tait," he found himself saying.

She laughed her self-deprecating, little laugh. "Oh, you have, Mr. Kendall. You'll find more than a few like me in any scullery in England."

He shook his head. On this point, he was certain. "*Like* you," he could allow. "But *you*? No. You are not a replaceable person, Miss Tait." He hesitated. "I must ask you one more question."

"By all means."

"What is it you want now?" He understood her dreams as a girl of sixteen years, but what were her dreams as the woman she was today?

Her smile turned sheepish. "You won't laugh?"

"Promise."

"The life I told you about? The one Tommy Trumble promised me? I still want it, foolish as that is. There's something I've never done."

"What is that?"

"I've walked across all manner of muck and filth in solid brown boots, but never across green grass on my bare feet. I would like to. I always thought it would be soft."

"It is," said Lucas. And he made a determination right there. "Will you agree to another day with me tomorrow?"

A wariness came over her. "Perhaps it would be best if we leave it with today."

She was protecting herself, he understood that and her need to. But he couldn't simply leave it.

He couldn't simply leave *her*.

This woman didn't understand something about herself that he did.

She was special.

"I have a surprise that I would like to show you."

"Another?" She shook her head in bemusement. "What is it?"

"Nice try, but it wouldn't be a surprise if I told you. Just say you will."

She thought it over. Every nerve in his body made itself known as he waited for her answer.

At last, she said, "No more mountains to climb?"

"I promise."

"Then, yes."

Relief arrowed through him.

Tomorrow, he would see this woman frolicking across green grass on her bare feet.

And he knew just the place.

6

Nell sat in the rented open-air cabriolet with a light breeze blowing through her hair and marveled that it was yet another bright, sunny day in the countryside. She knew it couldn't hold forever, but she would take what she could get of it.

Much like the man beside her.

She stole a sideways glance at Mr. Kendall. In truth, she was a little shy of him. She'd shared so much of her past yesterday. She'd shared what she'd never dared share with anyone. She would've thought he'd never want to see her again. But he hadn't reacted that way at all.

You are not a replaceable person, Miss Tait.

And then there were his words from the day before.

I don't see you that way.

The man kept saying words to her that no one else ever had. It was reason enough to be shy of him. Except there was another reason, too.

The kiss.

Perhaps it had started with him kissing her, but it had definitely ended with her kissing him and not wanting to stop. Tilly had been slanting sly looks her way all morning suggesting that the truth was writ plain. Of course, there had been the not-subtle waggle of Tilly's eyebrows, too.

Was it so obvious?

And yet another truth existed.

She was falling for him.

And she mustn't.

Her time with the man beside her, whose thigh jostled against hers with every rut in the road, was meant to be a lark. She would likely never see him again after today. In other words, now was no time to be shy.

If today was to be a lark, then she would give over to it.

"So, Mr. Kendall," she began.

He glanced at her, an easy smile curling about his mouth. "Yes, Miss Tait?"

"Oh, I think you can call me Nell by now."

"Would you like that?"

"Yes, I would."

"And would you consent to calling me Lucas?"

She laughed. She couldn't help herself.

"Are you laughing at my name?"

"You can be so formal and proper. You've truly been around nobs too long." She wondered if she should say what next came to mind and thought she should. "I like the name Lucas. It suits you."

"What is it you wanted to know?" he asked before adding, "*Nell.*"

"Where is the duke now?" A beat. "*Lucas.*"

"Oh, somewhere in the countryside," he said vaguely.

"And he doesn't need you?" Something about his relationship with his employer felt... *off*. One and one didn't make two, somehow.

"We have an understanding."

"And you're not afraid of losing your position?"

"Why would I be?" he asked, genuine curiosity in the glance he shot her.

She snorted. She couldn't help herself. "If my employers didn't need me, I'd be right worried they'd send me back to the East End, and I must admit I rather prefer Bond Street."

He nodded slowly. "Good point." He didn't elaborate further as he maneuvered the matched pair of horses into a smooth right turn that led onto a shaded lane, dueling colonnades of oaks to either side.

"This looks like someone's property," Nell observed.

"Indeed."

And it struck her. "This is the duke's estate."

"It is."

"Are we…" she began and stopped. But she had to know. "Are we trespassing?" she said in an urgent whisper, glancing around and not finding another soul.

"Not at all," said Lucas, utterly unconcerned.

They made another right turn, then a left, each new road narrower and less kept than the last. A river no wider than twenty feet appeared before them, and they turned right onto a road that more resembled a dirt trail that ran alongside the river, which in some places more resembled a creek. With the sun shining down, shallow water skimmed like glitter across the uneven riverbed. A rope swing hung from a tree, lazily swaying in the breeze. The river must've been deeper there. A swimming spot.

Effortlessly, Lucas tugged on the reins, and the horses came to a smooth stop at a lovely bend in the river, a willow tree near, low grass spread all the way to the riverbank.

Idyllic.

She'd seen that word in a book and had to look it up in the dictionary she kept near. *Full of natural charm. Picturesque.* She'd had to look that word up, too. But this place must've been in the mind of the person who'd dreamt up those words.

"What a pretty view," she said in her own words.

Lucas saw to the horses before joining her at the riverbank. "Today, I'm going to introduce you to two of my favorite pastimes."

"Oh?" she asked, watching him shake out a blanket and spread it flat.

He sat on the checked wool and pulled off his boots. "You must remove your boots and stockings before I tell you." He rolled up his trousers.

A bemused laugh escaped her. She could see there was no point in arguing, and why would she want to, anyway? She found a corner of the blanket and began unlacing her boots. What adventures she'd been having in these boots the last few days. When it came to her stockings, she would have to show a little leg. She snuck a peek toward Lucas. He'd returned to the cabriolet and was untying something from the back. It appeared to be a small basket, a bucket, and... two long poles?

"What is this, then?" she asked suspiciously.

"Have you ever fished?" he asked as he returned.

She screwed up her face and came to her bare feet. *"Fished?"* That answer was easy. "No."

His smile only widened. "Well, you are in for an afternoon of delight."

"I don't know about that." Not at all. "One of my brothers would go down to the Thames and catch eels with his bare hands."

"As..." Lucas looked utterly flummoxed. "...sport?"

Nell had no chance of stopping the chuckle that erupted from her. "To sell."

Lucas continued staring at her, blankly.

"To the pie man, of course," she explained.

"Of course," he said slowly.

"You've never had eel pie, have you?"

He spread his hands wide in a gesture of helplessness. "Alas, I haven't."

"Next time you're in London, you need to leave Mayfair and find yourself a pie shop in the East End. That's where you'll find the eel pies."

His smile fell an increment, and a sudden intensity formed about him. "I'll be in London next week." A hesitation. "And you?"

Like that, Nell went a bit breathless. "Aye. I shall."

"Perhaps you could take me to your favorite pie shop."

"Perhaps I could."

It wasn't settled—it wasn't yet definite—what they were saying below their words.

"You will?" he asked.

She swallowed. "I will."

There.

They'd each known what the other was saying.

And what the other wanted to hear.

This feeling that existed between them... It was new.

And she wanted more of it.

A FEELING SOARED THROUGH LUCAS.

Relief, yes.

Something else, too.

Joy.

"But, sadly," he said, "I must inform you there are no eels in this river."

He liked the way she smiled at his playful tone. "Thank heavens. Too many teeth on eels for my liking. What fish are in this river?"

"Brown trout like to run here. Now—" He had a delicate subject to broach. "There's a reason we had to re-move boots and stockings."

He glanced at the river, and her eyes went wide with understanding. "You don't mean..."

He nodded. "I do. We'll fish in our bare feet in the river. Best way to catch trout. So, you'll need to—" Here was the delicate subject. "Well, you see how I've rolled up my trousers..." He let the sentence trail, feeling heat suffuse his neck. He'd only just gotten her to agree to meet him in London next week, and now he risked offending her and he didn't want that.

The expression on her face turned quizzical. "Are you trying to tell me I need to tuck my dress into my drawers?"

Lucas cleared his throat. "Erm, yes."

She shook her head with amusement. "You know something?"

"What?"

"You do a right good imitation of a nob sometimes."

Lucas tried to smile and roll along with her observation, he really did, but it was difficult. For a variety of reasons. The first being that she was wrong in only a single respect. His wasn't an imitation.

Like the gentleman he was, he glanced away when she lifted the hem of her skirts. But that didn't prevent the periphery of his vision from snatching glimpses of her movements. The reveal of an ankle... the shapely length of a calf... He busied himself with tying a lure onto a line.

How fitting a metaphor.

He was completely hooked, wasn't he?

Once she'd gotten herself all sorted, he waved her over to his place at the riverbank. Gingerly, she stepped off the blanket, bare toes touching green grass. A smile utterly without design or consciousness spread across her face. The cool pleasure of grass blades was not lost on her. "That's what I thought it would feel like," she said.

He smiled, but kept quiet, not wanting to intrude on this moment. It was hers. That she could so appreciate something that he'd taken for granted his entire life filled him with a gravity he hadn't expected.

Her amber gaze met his. "You brought me here for this."

"Fishing? Yes."

"So I could walk barefoot on green grass."

"Ah, well, yes, that, too." He seemed to have lost the ability to form complete sentences.

"No one has ever done anything so thoughtful for me."

He tried to shrug off her appreciation. "It was quite a simple gesture, really."

"I think it's a grand one."

A moment stretched between them. One weighty with import. Import of what, Lucas couldn't say with absolute certainty. But he had an inkling, and just that inkling was enough to wallop him and steal the breath from his lungs.

And what he detected in her eyes?

She might have an inkling, too.

He held up a fishing pole. "Shall we?"

Hesitant, she nodded and followed him into the river. It was a shallow area, the water only reaching their ankles. He fixed her line and demonstrated how to cast. "Arm back, then forward with a flick of your wrist."

After a few tries, she got the knack of the casting motion, and minutes later they were fishing side by side, the sounds of water flowing... the shimmer of willow leaves... the song of a woodlark their only company.

"So, what makes a good fishing spot?" she asked, squinting into the water.

Lucas pointed to a place on the opposite side of the river. "See how it's deeper there? But it's shallow here?"

She nodded.

"Well, you want to lure them out of the deep and into the shallow, get them involved in the chase."

Before he could explain further, Nell's lure dipped and pulled taut. "Lawks," she exclaimed.

"Pull straight up," he said, wading over with the bucket. He grabbed the line and guided the trout in. Gently, so as not to harm the fish, he wrapped his hand around its scaly body, as the trout did its damnedest to wriggle free. "Would you like to hold your first catch?"

Nell looked dubious, but curious, too. "Is it slimy?"

"A little."

He wasn't expecting she would, but then she reached out. He slid the hook from the trout's mouth and held the fish out to her. "See how I'm holding it? That's how you'll want to do it. We don't want to harm him, because we'll be tossing him back."

She nodded and followed his instructions, handling the fish firmly but with care, and only emitting a few squeals when the fish gave a flurry of wiggles. "Now," he said, "let's wade to where it's a little deeper and set him down gently."

She did as instructed, and together they watched the trout swim toward freedom. She glanced over at him. "You're quite good at this."

"It's how I spent my childhood. There are few things I'd rather be doing at any given moment."

"Even with the squish of muck between your toes?" She scrunched her nose.

"Even with that," he said. It was only the truth. "Want to go again?"

"Strangely, I do."

He'd taken a few steps before he realized Nell wasn't beside him. He looked back and found her struggling to move. "It seems I've become tangled in the fishing line."

Lucas returned and began helping, turning her this way and that to follow the line that kept doubling back on itself in the wind that had suddenly kicked up, even crouching when it dipped into the water. He stood and reached around her, certain he would have her free in a matter of seconds. Then her face angled up, and he realized something. He had his arms around... *her*.

And she'd noticed.

With unspoken accord, she was lifting onto her toes and his face was lowering. In the next tick of time, their lips would touch. His blood ran hot in anticipation of that contact. Just as her breath whispered across his mouth, a heavy drop of rain landed *splat* on his nose, and Nell jumped. "What in the world?"

He glanced up to find a sky utterly transformed. Without them noticing, a slate-gray blanket of clouds had rolled in, threatening to unleash an unholy torrent of rain upon their heads. "We have about thirty seconds before—"

He wasn't able to finish the sentence before the weighty drops began plunking down on their heads with increasingly rapid succession. He'd just freed her of the line and secured the hook when the torrent unleashed. "We need to secure the horses," he shouted as he collected poles and bucket and began sloshing through the river toward the riverbank. He heard agreement at his back.

They gathered their things, and he stuck their boots in the bucket. "We won't be needing those?" Nell shouted, befuddled.

"I know of a place nearby," he said. He tossed everything onto the cabriolet bench, then ran to take the reins and settle the horses. "We walk."

She nodded, trusting.

So, it was he and Nell walked, barefoot, leading a pair of horses and their attached cabriolet through a summer rain shower. Though the day wasn't exactly ideal, it had certainly been made memorable.

Soon, the old groundskeeper's cottage came into view. It had long been empty of occupation, and was now where hunting and fishing gear were stored. A maid gave it a clean about once a month.

He pointed toward the front door. "You go inside while I settle the horses," he shouted. He could temporarily stable them in an old nearby barn.

When he finally entered the cottage, pausing in the doorway to shake rain off his overcoat and stomp mud off his bare feet, it was to find that Nell had busied herself by starting a fire in the hearth, and one in the little stove, too.

"Aren't you useful in a pinch?" he asked, removing his hat which had done naught to keep his hair from getting entirely soaked.

She glanced over her shoulder. "Benefit of making friends with a retired scullery maid."

Feeling a bit useless, he strode over to the small pantry in the corner and began gathering tea implements. He felt her watching him from the corner of her eye. A kettle… two chipped cups… a tin of leaves that were a decade old, if a day.

"Do you know what to do with those?" she asked.

"Approximately."

The admission stole a laugh from her. She was laughing at him, but he didn't mind. What sort of man didn't know how to make tea? The sort of man who'd had someone make his tea every day of his life.

A duke, for starters.

Right.

Nell crossed the room and dug into the basket he'd brought. "Ah," she said, her hand emerging with a jug of water. She dug around some more and found the luncheon he'd brought, too. "So, you're not completely without use."

"Damned with faint praise," he muttered.

As Nell took over the tea-making enterprise, Lucas dusted off a pair of chairs possessed of questionable upholstery before sitting in one and watching her, catching a glimpse of the sort of woman she must be at her work. *Quick. Efficient. Capable.*

"If I were to find myself stranded on an island in the middle of the ocean," he said, "I'd pick you for a companion."

Her light chuckle just reached him. She picked up the tea tray she'd assembled and brought it to the table beside the hearth. She reached out with a cup of black tea. The way he liked it. She'd remembered. She settled into the chair opposite him, and together they sipped in silence, the only sound the pitter-pat of rain on thatch.

But he noticed something *off* about Nell. Her hand possessed a subtle tremor when she lifted her teacup to her lips, which, actually, had become a shade of... "Your lips are turning purple. You're cold." He didn't ask. It was a statement of fact.

"Not very," she said, not very believably.

As they were as close to the fire as they could get without actually being inside the wide hearth, Lucas could see but one option. "You'll need to undress."

Her teacup froze halfway to her mouth. "Eh?"

"I may not be as useful in a pinch as you, but I do know this much. You need to undress to allow your clothes to dry." She wasn't going to agree. He could see it in the set of her jaw. "As do I." He hadn't planned on it, as his overcoat had protected him from getting entirely soaked, but he couldn't see her agreeing if he didn't.

"I can't go undressing," she said, as if to a child.

"Would you like to catch your death?" The question was on the dramatic side, but the possibility existed.

She stared at him. "Are you sure you aren't a nanny, instead of valet?"

He had sounded a mite hysterical, but he wouldn't relent. His fingers began working the knot of his cravat to prove his seriousness and intent. Stunned expression on her face, she watched, as if mesmerized by his movements. "Well, get to it," he said.

If that sounded less nanny and more duke, so be it. The woman needed to get out of those clothes.

"I can't be running around here in the buff, now can I?" she asked, incredulous. "This isn't the Sandwich Islands."

Fair point. He snorted and tossed her a blanket. "Any other requirements?"

"Turn around."

He did as bid, his ears attuned to the sounds of her movement at his back as he removed shirt and trousers before cloaking himself in a musty woolen blanket that the moths had taken a liking to, judging by the number of holes.

"You can turn around now."

He pivoted and found her wrapped in the gray blanket, her bare toes peeking out. She extended her hand and waggled her fingers. "Hand them over."

Lucas extended his damp clothes and watched as she draped them all about the hearth. They would be dry in no time at all. He wasn't sure he liked that idea. He wanted more time with her, not less.

"I'm not much use, am I?" he asked.

"Some, I suppose," she said, saucy. "The Duke must keep you around for a reason."

Lucas held his silence. Lie after lie kept stacking up. Soon, they would form a wall too high to see over. And that wall would be impenetrable if he let it happen.

He must tell her his true identity, for what was budding between them held substance.

"You know what I told you yesterday?" she asked, sliding a glance toward him from beneath her eyelashes. "About my dream of a cottage in the country?"

"Yes." The conversation had occupied the majority of his waking thoughts since.

"This cottage is exactly what I pictured."

How unaffected she was. For him, this old gamekeeper's cottage was a useful structure, but mostly an afterthought. For her, she looked at this place and saw a dream unrealized.

"It's silly."

He shook his head. "It's not."

"I'm an East End girl, and that was a fantasy. Though..." She let the rest of the sentence trail.

"Though?"

"Though, here with us, right now, fantasy is reality, isn't it?" Somehow, the question emerged both shy and bold.

Could she be hinting at what he thought she was? He went very still so as not to startle possibility away.

"And you, well..." Again, her sentence trailed.

"What about me?"

"You're the sort of man a woman could see sharing a cottage with."

"Like fantasy?"

"Exactly like that."

The look in her eyes... the content of her words... She was, indeed, saying exactly what he thought she was.

He shifted forward on his chair. "But here's the thing you need to know," he said, low, intent.

"Yes?"

"I'm a man of flesh and blood. Quite real, in fact." Should he ask the question on the tip of his tongue? *Yes.* "Would you like to find out just how real?"

She took a step forward, then another, the tail of her blanket dragging across the floor behind her, until mere inches separated them. "For a rainy afternoon?"

He reached up and caressed the side of her face. "What is one to do on a rainy afternoon but find pleasure indoors?"

Her gaze remained steady on his. "Is that what you're offering? Pleasure?"

"If you'll allow me."

She swallowed and moved closer. He spread his legs, and she stepped between, letting her blanket fall away. Her lissome, naked body bathed in golden light from the hearth, desire and permission shone in her eyes, and Lucas knew.

This wasn't about a single afternoon's pleasure.

This was the beginning of forever.

7

*P*leasure.

Nell had been made many promises by a man, but never that.

And the intent look in this man's eyes said he could deliver.

A shiver traced through her. Not from the chill in the air, but from a desire so strong her knees went weak with it.

He shrugged off his blanket, and the sight before her froze her in place. *Golden... gorgeous... Greek god...* From his broad shoulders and thick thighs to the trail of blond hair that led down his muscled chest and ridged stomach to his—*oh*—manhood, long and rigid and—*oh*—ready. A pulsing sensation shot straight through her.

His hand slid around to cup the nape of her neck and draw her forward, toward his upturned mouth, and she understood something elemental... something that made what she was about to do *right*.

This was on her own terms.

This—what existed between him and her—wasn't about empty promises of a future.

It was honest.

It was about the here and now.

And, here and now, she wanted this man.

Just before her lips met his, she took a sip of air. *Sandalwood... Man.* "Mmm," she moaned. This man smelled so good.

Then his mouth claimed hers, and he palmed the small of her back, bringing her forward so she pressed up against him, his body hot against hers. His tongue slipped between her lips and met hers in a tangle, and of a sudden, she was ravenous for him—her hands sliding through his tousled hair, across his shoulders, down arms hard with muscle. He plucked the pins from her hair, allowing it to fall in a curtain to her waist. "Why do you hide this glorious mane from the world?" he muttered against her mouth.

Nell couldn't clearly think why at the moment, but was mostly certain it had something to do with propriety. Then his hands found her bottom and pressed her so close only a thin sheen of sweat separated them. The feel of his skin on hers... the wild beat of his heart mirroring hers... the ragged in and out of his breath... She'd never felt this intensity, this *intimacy*, with another.

Pulled along by instinct, she placed her hands on his shoulders, and lifted one leg, then the other, coming to straddle him on the chair, her mouth never releasing his, her quim slick against the hard, heavy press of his manhood. Without conscious thought, she moved against him, luxuriating in his thick rigidity against her softness.

Oh, how she wanted—*needed*—him inside her.

He shifted back, breaking the kiss, eliciting a displeased moan from her. His serious blue gaze met hers. "Are you certain?"

"Oh, yes," she said without a moment's hesitation, wrapping her legs around his waist to make her intentions unquestionably clear, in the event they weren't already.

She slid along the length of his manhood, pulling a long, rumbly, "Oh," from him. "Do that again," he said against her mouth.

She swiveled her hips, and sensation rippled through her unlike any she'd ever experienced. What she'd done with Tommy Trumble, in haylofts and once in the back of a wagon, was nothing to *this*.

Lucas's mouth found a place on her neck, just below her ear, and he licked, his tongue a velvety glide against her, sending shivers purling up her spine. Down his kisses trailed until his capable mouth found one breast and his hand the other. He licked, sucked, squeezed, nipped at the cherry-hard nubs, driving her mindless with pleasure and need. Her hand trailed down his body until it reached that which she sought... his thick, hard manhood. She took his heavy length in hand, giving him a testing squeeze and stroke. Her mouth found his ear. "I need this."

Large, capable hands squeezed her bottom and lifted enough that he pressed against the entrance of her sex. She held above him, poised to take him inside, anticipation running riot through her, filling her every secret place. Then, her eyes locked onto his, their blue gone dark and cloudy with desire, and she took him in inch by sublime inch, his thickness stretching her, filling her, discomfort balanced by exquisite pleasure.

"Oh, Lucas," poured from her in a long animal moan as he clutched and began to move her on him, slowly, with intention, every movement delivering a fresh wave of pleasure.

His mouth met the whorl of her ear. "Am I too much for you?"

She shook her head and clutched him closer, her body so small against his larger one, but so perfectly fitted, too. Sweat beading down the side of his face, between the cleft of her breasts, primal recognition flowed between them. This coupling wasn't merely of the body. She felt it down to the marrow of her bones, to the core of her soul. Theirs was a joining of the spirit and possibly of another place, too—a place deep in her chest, a place she'd vowed no man would ever touch again.

His hips found a new rhythm, and she could no longer think. All she could do was... *feel... him...* taking her over completely as his hand reached between their bodies and his thumb found a place—*oh*—a place along her quim she hadn't known existed as he used her slickness to graze the nub even as he moved in and out of her.

All she could do was hold on—and possibly whimper and very likely softly scream—as he delivered on his promise of pleasure, tempting forward a feeling... a coiling tension concentrated in her sex—in the very place he rubbed with his thumb, that he penetrated with his manhood—so that she only existed there.

"Nell," he murmured in her ear. "We're close, my sweet. Come with me."

"Where?" she was only able to ask on a quick exhale, her breath coming in gasps.

A low, rumbly chuckle sounded deep in his chest. "You'll see," he said on a thrust that should've been too hard, but wasn't. It only made her want another and another and—*oh*—another. She'd become a being transformed, insatiable for him, as she sought and strained for the place he promised. Then his thumb increased its pressure against her, and his manhood delivered a deliberate thrust and her body teetered on the edge of... of... of... before fragmenting into a million starlit pieces, her quim pulsing its release around him in butterfly flickers, pleasure taking wing through her veins to every nerve ending.

Head arced back, he stroked in and out of her once... twice... before lifting her off him and taking his release in his hand, his gaze fixed upon her in a way that made her breathless all over again. Here it was, the feeling of intimacy. She understood why he spilled his seed outside of her, and felt, strangely, both grateful and deprived.

He reached for the blanket and dried himself before pulling her to him and settling back into the armchair. The side of her face against his chest, she picked up the slowing beat of his heart, a pace that matched hers as her body began slowly piecing itself together again.

"I, um," she began and stopped. Perhaps it was better not to say.

He lazily stroked her hair. "What is it?"

Oh, his caress felt so good on top of everything else that had just made her feel *so* good. Which was likely why she found herself finishing the sentence. "I never knew it could feel like that."

"Like what?"

"So... sublime."

It was the truth. But maybe not the full truth.

The full truth involved more than sensation of the body. But sensation that tapped deeper than mere physical surfaces.

Sensation that had no business existing between them.

Or... did it?

"I thought this would be a bit of fun," she found herself confessing.

"You're not having fun?"

"It feels like more."

AND IN THAT INSTANT LUCAS DECIDED IT WAS TIME.

He pitched forward and set a startled Nell on her feet. "Let us dress. Our clothes should be dry by now." Or dry enough. "I have something to tell you."

"What is it?"

He shook his head. "Not here." He stood and jerked his trousers up his legs. With half an assessing eye upon him, she followed his lead. She was wondering about him.

Fair enough.

The time had arrived.

He must tell her the truth about himself. Not here, but half a mile away. In the ducal manor house. It had to be there. It was his only chance to keep her. Not because she would fall for him like every unmarried lady in London because of his title. It was for the opposite reason, in fact.

When he told her the truth about his identity, she needed to see he was the same man in the large house as he was in this tiny cottage.

For here was what he understood about the small, remarkable woman currently lacing up her soggy boots: Rather than accept him for his title of duke, she would reject him for it.

And here was what she needed to understand: He was the man who loved her.

Loved?

Surprise at the realization traced through him. But that didn't mean it was untrue. He loved this small, remarkable woman. All this time, she was the woman he'd been searching for. The wife he'd wanted.

Now, all he had to do was convince her to be with him despite his title.

Once they'd both sufficiently dressed, he grabbed her pelisse and held it out. After a slight hesitation, she allowed him to assist her.

"Shall we?" he asked and reached for her hand.

She cut him a smile that was equal parts self-aware and shy. After what they'd just done, what was one hand holding another?

An intimacy.

An acknowledgement that more than coupling bound them.

Outside, the rain shower had disappeared as quickly as it had arrived. Birds sang and twittered about trees still dripping heavy droplets of rain past. The sun shone low and yellow in a clear blue sky, preparing for the coming of dusk.

"The air smells so *bright*," said Nell. "Of sun and grass and rain. We don't get air like this in London."

Together, they led the horses out of the barn, and Lucas helped Nell up onto the cabriolet's bench. Bedraggled and—dare he think it?—*happy*, they sat side by side as he drove them through the estate.

"Can you give me a hint as to where we're going?" she asked.

"I'm going to show you a house."

Just then they topped a gentle hill, and Amherst House came into view. Wide eyes rounded on him. "*That's* what you're calling a house?"

"Aye," he said simply.

She shook her head on a little snort. "You've been living among aristocrats too long." She pointed toward the massive, centuries-old Peak Moor sandstone structure. "*That* is a castle."

"The family call it the manor house."

Nell cut him a skeptical glance. "Let's meet in the middle with palace."

He laughed. He couldn't help it. He loved her point of view. He loved...

Her.

As they rolled to a stop in front of Amherst House,

Nell's awe of the place hadn't abated one bit. "And this is where you grew up?"

"It is."

She nodded slowly and seemed to make up her mind about something.

"What is it?"

"It's no wonder you have a few airs."

He handed her down from the cabriolet and guided her up the wide stone staircase that led to the grand front entrance. Without hesitation, he pushed open the ten-foot-high oak door and stepped into the receiving hall with Nell at his side. Her brow lifted toward the thirty-foot ceiling. "The duke won't mind us entering through the front door?"

He shook his head, determined to speak no more false words to this woman.

"What about the servants?"

"I'm known to all."

A chambermaid entered the hall, humming a soft tune. Upon noticing him and Nell, she stopped abruptly, dipped in a flustered curtsy, and scurried out of sight. Nell's eyebrows drew together. "Maids curtsy to valets in this house?" She spoke the word *house* with no small amount of irony.

"Nell, there is something you need to know about me."

"Oh, I'd say I know a great deal," she said, a light blush staining her cheeks and a saucy smile curling about her mouth.

"I'm not exactly who you think I am."

Her brow crinkled, her smile fading into a memory of itself. "Pardon?"

"I am in the ways that matter, but—"

"*Lucas?*" came a faraway voice from on high.

It was only then he noticed that all the chandeliers

were lit. And they shouldn't have been, because he'd been away and shouldn't have returned for a week.

Nell questioned him with her gaze before swinging around to find a woman bedecked to the hilt in no fewer than five varieties of jewels standing at the head of the wide staircase that elegantly curved to the second floor.

Mama.

And behind her arrived yet more of his family. Elizabeth and Catherine, his two older sisters, and their husbands—the Earl of Chandos and Baron Shomberg. Lucas had no notion of the men's first names as they went exclusively by their titles. Rather high in the instep for his own preference, but his brothers-in-law seemed to make his sisters happy.

Nell's puzzlement was quickly transforming into horror, the color draining from her face. "Lucas," she muttered, low, so only he could hear. "What is this?"

Clearly, Mama was wondering the exact same thing. "What are *you* doing *here*, Lucas? Baron Hatton sent word that you never arrived. So, we came up from London early. I was considering sending out a search party if we didn't hear from you on the morrow." The statement, however, lacked any urgency. All usually worked out for the best in his mother's world, and it was with that expectation that she approached life. Her gaze shifted and landed on Nell. "And why is my dressmaker here, too?"

Nell was his mother's dressmaker?

Blast.

Matters had gone from bad to worse.

Nell dipped in a shallow curtsy. "Your Grace." Her gaze rounded on Lucas, knowledge shining in outraged eyes. "*You* are the Duke? You're not his valet?"

"*Valet?*" asked Mama on a harrumph. "My son refuses to employ a valet. Says he knows how to dress himself with perfect competency."

Nell looked poised to bolt down the driveaway with nary a glance back. And who could blame her? Instinctively, subtly, Lucas's fingers felt for hers at his side. She avoided his touch by clasping her hands before her.

Mama began descending the staircase. "Oh, I see."

"You do?" Lucas and Nell asked at the same time.

Mama's attention remained fixed on Nell. "*You* thought we were to have our dressmaking sessions at Amherst House. While *I* was under the impression we would meet on the morrow in Matlock Bath. After all, I am in dire need of a few spa days."

"Well, I, erm," stammered Nell.

Mama waved away the supposed mix-up. "No matter, you're here now. Send for your luggage to be brought in, and we'll have our session here come morning. Then I'll be off to Matlock Bath for my spa sessions. The waters are truly healing."

Nell's cheeks were flaming. Though it was Lucas's instinct to jump to her defense, he held back, understanding he shouldn't. Better that Mama continued with her misinterpretation of the situation until he could get Nell alone.

"I don't have my luggage with me," said Nell.

Mama's brow lifted. "No? Well, I don't see the point in that."

"Her bags were stowed on the wrong carriage," said Lucas. He had to say something of use. "They'll be in Scotland by now."

"Oh, dear. And how did you come across her, Lucas?"

"By the side of the road." Everyone aimed questioning eyes at him. "Her coach was beset by highwaymen."

"*Highwaymen?*" exclaimed Mama, incredulous. "I

thought they died out with the last century. Anyway, what incredibly bad luck you've had, my dear. Well, no help for it. You must be given a hot bath, and, Elizabeth, you're of a similar size. You'll lend her a gown of yours."

"Of course," said Elizabeth.

Lucas's sisters and their husbands were glancing back and forth between Lucas and Nell, skepticism writ clear across their faces. They were wary of the lost-luggage-highwaymen tale. But they showed no offense. They were, if anything, amused. His sisters always did derive a bit too much pleasure from watching him scramble out of a scrape.

"And you must join us for our evening meal, Nell."

"Miss Tait," said Lucas, without thinking.

Mama's eyes widened. "Pardon?" No one naysayed a duchess.

Except a duke.

"She should be addressed as Miss Tait," he said, firm, as only a duke could.

"Ah, of course."

He wasn't finished. "And she should be asked if *she* would like to join us for the evening meal."

"Quite right, Lucas," said Mama. She returned her attention to Nell. "Miss Tait, would you like to join us for evening tea?"

All eyes upon her, Lucas thought Nell might shrink. But she didn't. Rather, she gathered herself with a quiet dignity, looked the Dowager Duchess of Amherst square in the eye, and spoke the most shocking word Lucas would ever hear. "*Yes.*" A beat. "It would be my pleasure, Your Grace."

In an instant, Mama took over and was directing servants to assist Miss Tait, who was suddenly swept up the staircase and gone.

But not before one last parting glance at Lucas. He'd

never known a single glance, caught for the fraction of a second, could communicate so much. *Shock. Befuddlement. Anger.* Truly, he would think all lost if not for one fact.

She'd agreed to stay. For a while longer, at least.

Which gave him precious time.

Which meant all wasn't lost.

A chance—slender though it was—remained.

8

Nell moved through the next hour of her life as if someone had stuck a great wad of cotton in her brain.

She couldn't form a single clear thought. They all kept tumbling about and landing in a jumble.

So, she allowed herself to be led. Up the grand, curved staircase... into a pale lavender bedroom bedecked with tapestries and velvet... into a white-tiled bathing room... into a bathing tub the size of a small pond, where she soaked—luxuriated, really—until the water began to cool. Then she was slipping into a dress of pale-yellow silk. A dress like a breath of sunshine.

She'd never worn one of her creations, wary of developing a taste for luxury. And, now, feeling the sumptuous slide of silk against her skin, she understood she'd been correct. One could easily get a taste for this.

She gave herself a long once-over before the full-length mirror. With this dress, matching slippers, and white satin gloves that reached above her elbows, she would look like a lady to all the world beyond these four walls.

And how had this come to pass?

The cotton cleared from her brain.

Because of *him*. The man she'd thought a valet, who was, in fact, a duke.

Tears of hurt and anger threatened.

She'd been duped by a man, again.

How had she let that happen?

She'd gotten ahead of herself... *again*... and seen a future.

Truly, it had been so easy. For here was the thing: A dressmaker and a valet? They could have a future together.

But a dressmaker and a duke?

No future lay there.

Only a bit of fun.

His bit of fun.

That was all she'd been to him.

Oh, what a fool she.

Part of her wanted to find a hole in the ground and sink into it. But she'd never listened to that voice, and she wasn't about to start today. She'd come to this part of England with a job to do, because, impossibly, the duke's mother happened to be one of *Galante: Dressmakers Extraordinaire*'s best clients.

She wouldn't lose a valuable client over this bit of foolishness. She may have lost a man and a future that was never real, but she didn't have to lose all.

"Face the world with a smile on yer mouth. Even when it kicks you in the teeth. 'Specially then."

Even if behind that smile her heart ached, no one had to know. Wasn't that what smiles were for anyway?

So, it was with a smile on her face that Nell was led through the sprawling castle. She didn't care what Lucas... *the Duke of Amherst*... said. This "house" was a castle.

When she finally arrived in the dining room, which was surely lit by no fewer than one hundred candles, casting shadows onto gleaming sterling silver service and prisms through cut crystal, the family were already seated. The men rose at her arrival. She most decidedly tried to avoid Lucas—oh, it was impossible to think of him as a duke—but she couldn't help herself. He was dressed in evening black and looking every inch the dashing duke, with his tousled blond hair, easy smile, and sparkling blue eyes.

Actually, she detected no small amount of concern in those eyes and a corresponding tightness about his smile.

But she wouldn't think about that.

Not now.

She had a lifetime for those regrets.

How had she not seen him for the aristocrat he so clearly was?

Because she hadn't wanted to.

That was the plain truth.

Because a dressmaker didn't have a future with a duke.

Because a dressmaker could have a future with a valet, and she'd allowed herself to want it—to believe in it.

Fool.

The nearest footman—she'd counted no fewer than four—pulled out a chair for her, and she slid into it. She found herself seated with a lord to either side, presumably the husbands of Lucas's sisters, the Ladies Elizabeth and Catherine, who were, of course, also Nell's clients. The ladies sat on the opposite side of the wide mahogany table, with the Dowager Duchess at one end and Lucas at the other.

Nell had harbored the idea that she could slip unnoticed into her seat and partake of the meal that would surely taste like dust in her mouth, invisibility being a particular skill of hers. However, that skill appeared to be failing her tonight as all eyes fell on her.

"Miss Tait," said the Dowager Duchess, even as she signaled the servants to begin serving the evening meal. "I hope you found your room to your satisfaction."

A bowl of soup appeared before Nell. "Um, yes, quite," she said, distracted by the pale orange color. Carrot soup?

She made to pick up a spoon so as to satisfy her curiosity, but she found no fewer than three to choose from. *Three.* Who needed three spoons to eat a bowl of soup? The answer to that was easy. *Aristocrats.*

A footman appeared at her side, cutting between her and one of the lords as he leaned forward to adjust the candelabra. "Start from the outside and work your way in with each course," he said, quiet, discreet, and then he was gone.

Nell counted three spoons, three forks, and two knives. How many courses were there to be anyway?

Even so, relief spiked through her. She could do this. She could survive an evening meal with a family of aristocrats.

Unable to ignore the heat of Lucas's gaze on the side of her face a moment longer, she flicked him a glance. Something shone within those hazy blue depths. *Knowledge.* He'd sent the footman with those instructions.

A feeling wanted to well up inside her. *Gratitude.*

Another feeling, too.

One she'd experienced only this afternoon for Mr. Lucas Kendall, valet. A feeling that had felt safe and... *right.*

But His Grace Lucas Kendall, the Duke of Amherst...

She didn't know how to feel about *him.*

If he was expecting her to melt into a puddle of thankfulness, it would be a long wait.

Still, it was with a smile on her face that she pivoted

away from him and toward the Dowager Duchess when the lady asked, "And I suppose the Galante sisters know how fortunate they are to have secured your dressmaking talents for their Bond Street shop?" She delicately sipped a spoonful of soup. "Truly, in all my years, I've never seen finer stitchwork than yours, Miss Tait."

Irritatingly, Nell felt the flood of a hot blush staining her cheeks, pinking the tips of her ears. "'Tis I who was the lucky one to have secured a place with them, Your Grace." It was the absolute truth.

As only a duchess could, the woman waved the idea away. "Oh, pish, you're being too modest."

"Well," began Lady Elizabeth, "one thing you can say about the Galante sisters."

Lady Catherine finished her sister's thought. "They certainly know how to marry well."

Nell detected no snobbishness in the statement, but rather admiration. In fact, though a family of the highest social standing in England, they seemed rather nice. She'd always thought so when they visited the shop, but now she had it confirmed. She couldn't help stealing another glance at Lucas. He was one of them. She might have to allow that he was nice, too. Which only confused matters further. How could he be a nice man and lie to her for days?

"The second son of a duke and a French marquis? I'll say," added the Dowager Duchess, after another sip of soup.

Though Nell detected no negativity toward Isabel and Eva Galante—now Lady Percival Bretagne and the Marquise de Touraine, respectively—she felt the need to defend them. "'Tis their husbands who married well," she said.

Five sets of brows lifted toward her. Aristocratic brows.

Her blush had most assuredly reached her toes by now.

The only one in the room who refrained from raising a brow was Lucas. Instead, he sat back in his chair and quietly regarded her, head cocked, eyes slightly narrowed. In some intangible way, she sensed he was willing her to say more—whatever was on her mind.

The very notion steeled her to step outside the comfort of invisibility and into the fray. "In addition to being talented women of business, Isabel and Eva are kind and intelligent and strong. They took me in when I had no family and made me theirs."

She hadn't intended to say so much, but now that she'd done it, she hadn't a single regret. She wouldn't think about how the impressed look in Lucas's eyes made her feel. Perhaps it was the soup—which had turned out to be summer squash—that warmed her.

"Well said, my dear," proclaimed the Dowager Duchess. "You're not only a talented dressmaker, but a loyal friend, too. That speaks well of your character."

Nell's smile might have faltered at the praise, but it held.

Once the empty soup bowls were replaced with a plate of fish filet, smothered in a delicate white sauce with a dish of asparagus on the side, Lady Elizabeth cleared her throat pointedly. "Now, Lucas, you must tell us where you ran off to these last three days. Mama has been able to talk of little else."

"My guess was London," said Lady Catherine, picking up a strange knife that must've been for this course. Nell followed her lead.

"Not London," said Lucas, curt.

"See?" said Lady Elizabeth to the room at large. "He wouldn't go up to Town." A mischievous smile tipped about her mouth. "My guess was that you'd run away to the circus. You always did have a liking for the travelers who came through with the seasons."

Lucas swiped his napkin across his mouth, clearly irritated with his siblings, who wore the triumphant, meddling expressions of older sisters toying with their younger brother.

"If you must know," he said, "on the road to Baron Hatton's estate, my horse threw a shoe and I had to have her reshod."

As one, Lady Elizabeth and Lady Catherine's eyes narrowed. Their sisterly noses sensed withheld information. Their brother would yield it, their expressions said.

Watching Lucas squirm... Nell couldn't help but find it fun.

"And where was this?" asked Lady Elizabeth.

"Matlock Bath," said Lucas.

Lady Catherine's gaze rounded on Nell. "Isn't that where you've been staying, Miss Tait?" she asked, all innocence and anything but.

It was no longer fun.

For the Dowager Duchess's part, the innuendo underlying the conversation—*thankfully*—seemed to have passed her by entirely. "Perhaps you can try again tomorrow, Lucas, and take a spare horse or two with you."

Lucas stabbed his trout with more force than was strictly necessary. "I have no intention of visiting Baron Hatton tomorrow, or the next day, or any day, in fact," he said with the studied calm that spoke of a storm beneath.

The Dowager Duchess's fork clattered to her plate. "Now you're breaking another engagement?"

Nell's eyebrows drew together. *Another engagement?* Was the man an outright menace to unbetrothed women?

85

Carefully—too carefully—Lucas placed his utensils on his plate. "There can be no engagement when one hasn't even met the young lady in question."

The Dowager Duchess harrumphed, unwilling to concede the point. "It wasn't so long ago that there would've been."

"Thankfully, we live in the nineteenth century, and such marriages no longer happen."

The sisters tittered, positively gleeful to see their brother twisting in the wind. Meanwhile, their husbands tucked into their meals.

"And yet," said Nell, instantly regretting opening her mouth and yet unable not to, "there was one broken engagement."

The statement wasn't phrased as a question, but Lucas would know it for one. The full brunt of his gaze met hers. "There was."

He hesitated, gathering his next words. Nell clutched the napkin in her lap, knuckles white, as she waited, breath held. His next words shouldn't matter, but they did.

"It was agreed by all," he continued, "and most particularly by the lady in question, that we didn't suit. No hard feelings were left behind, and the matter was quickly resolved, Lady Dorothea's reputation entirely intact."

Nell shouldn't, but she believed him. The earnestness in his eyes… It was genuine.

"She recently became betrothed to the eldest son of the Duke of Bolton," said Lady Elizabeth.

"Almost as good as a sitting duke, I suppose," added Lady Catherine.

Lady Elizabeth returned her feline smile to Lucas. She wasn't finished toying with him yet. "Do you know what they call you in London, dear brother?"

"I reckon you'll tell me."

"The Farmer Duke," supplied Lady Catherine.

"As a matter of fact," he said, wearily, "I had heard that one."

The Dowager Duchess lost her patience with this line of conversation. "Honestly, son, whom are you going to marry?"

Nell couldn't understand why the question made the breath catch in her throat. Whom this man married was none of her concern.

Not anymore.

Not since he revealed he was a duke an hour or so ago.

And yet when his gaze shifted and met hers, her breath refused to dislodge.

"I'm hoping someone will have me."

She might never draw breath again.

LUCAS KNEW HE SHOULD RELEASE NELL'S GAZE, BUT HE wanted this to be absolutely, without-a-doubt clear to her.

He was speaking to her.

She needed to understand that.

The words he'd spoken to her this afternoon, they were only the beginning. He wanted to expand on them. *Here... now.* Even in front of his family. If this was his only chance, he would stop at nothing. She was the only woman for him, and he'd known this afternoon— at the river... inside the cottage—she'd felt the same about him.

But, then, he'd been a valet.

Now he was a duke.

One who had hidden his identity from her.

A liar and a duke.

He wasn't sure which was worse in her estimation.

"Well," said Mama, allowing her empty plate to be replaced by the main course of leg of lamb, "any bride of yours will need to be utterly enamored of the country."

"That has certainly been established," said Elizabeth, the more mischievous of his two sisters. "Isn't that correct, Farmer Duke?"

He couldn't help smiling. Even when Elizabeth was wreaking the most havoc upon him, it was always done with a light, loving touch.

"Shall we go out into the fields and pluck out a farmer's daughter for you?" asked his mother, exasperated. "Truly, Lucas."

"I'm not sure we'll have to go that far," said Lucas, stealing a glance at Nell, who was staring down at her roast lamb as if it were the most fascinating joint of meat she'd ever laid eyes upon. The twin blushes staining her cheeks gave her away, though. She was listening most intently. "She will need to be pretty."

"Of course, she'll need to be pretty," said Catherine, with an unladylike snort. "You're a man, aren't you? But what of her accomplishments? How many languages would you like her to speak?"

"One," said Lucas. "English, preferably."

"Now don't be too hasty, Amherst," said Lord Chandos, Elizabeth's husband. "You might consider the advantages of a wife who speaks a different language."

This drew a hearty laugh from the room, and a lighthearted, "Oh, you insufferable man," from his wife.

"Should she play an instrument?" asked Catherine. Her interrogation wasn't finished. "Night can be long in the country without sufficient entertainments."

"The sounds of crickets and frogs will do." Lucas tried to recapture Nell's eye and failed.

"What about a lady who can paint?"

Lucas shrugged. He didn't know if Nell spoke a

dozen languages, could paint, or play an instrument, and he didn't care.

"Oh, Lucas," said Mama—her exasperation with her only son had grown over the duration of the meal. "Do you even care if she can read?"

He tapped forefinger to mouth. "Yes, I'd like that."

Mama's eyes narrowed on him, as if a distasteful idea had just struck. "Have you been reading novels?" she asked suspiciously. "They will give you ideas if you're not careful."

This drew another round of laughter from the room.

"What other accomplishments?" asked Catherine once the laughter had died down.

"She would need to want a large number of children."

"The creation of a large family is hardly an accomplishment," said Elizabeth with a sly smile. "It simply requires, ahem, diligence."

"Elizabeth!" exclaimed Mama, shocked by her eldest daughter, who simply shrugged a shoulder.

At last, Nell lifted her gaze and unerringly found his. He'd been describing her all this time, and the look in her eyes said she knew it. But he needed to say more.

And here was his chance.

It might be his only one.

He held her warm amber gaze and spoke his heart. "My wife will have grit and tenacity. She will know her own mind. She will find the humor in life. Even if she got splashed with mud in the high street and her favorite frock was ruined, she would see the silliness in it and laugh."

"I'm afraid you'll find no such woman, my brother," said Catherine with dry certainty.

He continued speaking directly to Nell. Her eyes, wide and unflinching, remained locked onto his, yet they gave nothing of her inner thoughts away. He must keep trying. "She will see *me*. Not the duke, but the man. The man who loves her." His heart beat hard and fast against his ribs, threatening to race out of his chest. He had yet more to say. "That's the woman I'll marry. If she'll have me."

The room's breath held. All had caught on to whom Lucas was addressing, five sets of eyes flicking back and forth between him and Nell. Time, too, seemed to have understood, as if recognizing it couldn't proceed until she'd given her answer.

On a sudden flurry of movement, Nell's chair scraped back and she shot to her feet. "Your Grace," she began, addressing Mama. Her chest was heaving, and she sounded slightly out of breath. That made two of them. "Thank you for your thoughtful hospitality, but I'm afraid I must"—her gaze caught his for a quick second—"go."

"Do you have a megrim?" asked Mama. "The Duchess of Arundel, a dear friend of mine, has given me the recipe for her special megrim tonic. I'll have Cook whip it up and sent to your room."

Nell swallowed, the elegant column of her throat undulating with the movement. "I shall be leaving." Though her voice shook, it was definite.

"But it's night, my dear," said Mama, as if that settled it.

But Nell wasn't so easily soothed. "I must return to Matlock Bath."

Mama laughed without malice. "Well, that's ridiculous."

Seeing that neither woman would be swayed, Lucas shot to his feet and was already moving. "I'll assist you."

"Not *you*," said Nell over her shoulder, her pale-yellow skirts swishing in her wake.

Lucas wasn't so easily dissuaded from his pursuit.

"*Lucas,*" said Mama, imperious, stopping him in his tracks. "We need a word. *Alone.*"

Lucas glanced around the room and found his sisters regarding him with lifted brows and curious, little smiles on their mouths. Their husbands seemed mostly indifferent to the drama. For his part, Lucas followed Mama into the study that overlooked the front lawn. She pivoted and pinned him with the motherly stare that told him he wouldn't be leaving until he'd outed with the truth.

"What is this all about, Lucas?"

9

I f it was the truth his mother wanted, Lucas decided
it was the truth she would have. He was done with
games.

"I intend to marry Miss Tait."

Mama went stone still, the only movement on her
person the narrowing of her piercing blue eyes. "You
intend to marry my dressmaker?"

"If she will have me. Do you take issue with that?"
The question emerged more combative than was
strictly fair, but he wasn't tolerating a speck of opposi-
tion from his family. They might as well know it from
the outset.

"Considering how only minutes ago I was plotting
to pluck a farmer's daughter from fields for you, you
should know that I don't," said Mama. "Besides, Lucas
—and I know you have a tendency to forget this about
yourself—you are a duke, and although this marriage
will likely put you beyond the pale socially for a time,
you can marry whom you like."

He deserved that. But the harmony of his family
mattered to him, so he must ask another question. His
mother's answer wouldn't change the intention of his
heart, but it would provide an idea of what he would be

dealing with in the years to come, if by some miracle Nell consented to be his wife. "You do like her, don't you?"

Mama reached out and squeezed his hand. He sensed a softening. "I do. She isn't noble born, but she has a gentility about her. I'm certain I shall come to love her in short order." She said it so matter-of-factly Lucas didn't doubt her. His mother might've been a duchess, but she possessed a heart willing to believe the best in people. "Further," she continued, "I think you and she shall suit."

And here it was—his mother's blessing. He hadn't needed it, but he'd wanted it.

Which left but one obstacle.

"Now, I must convince her."

Of a sudden, Mama's head canted to an awkward left angle, her eyes narrowed on a point over his shoulder. "You'll have to catch her first."

Lucas swung around and located what had captured her attention.

Nell—wearing her own damp clothes, marching down the driveway, fire in her step.

He was already halfway to the door when Mama called out, "Do you know what you'll say to her?"

"No," he admitted, stopping in his tracks. He only knew he couldn't let her leave, not yet, but he hadn't the faintest idea how to keep her.

Mama closed the distance between them, working and twisting the ring on her right pinky until it slid off. "This should be about her size."

The ring she extended toward him was gold with delicate engraved roses twining around, and nothing like the more ostentatious ones populating her other fingers. He'd never known his mother to remove it.

"Your father gave me this ring very early on in our courtship," she said, wistfulness in her voice. "Not as a formal proposal of marriage, but as a promise that what we had together was genuine and only between us. All the pomp and circumstance of a future duke marrying a marquess's daughter would come later. This ring was a reminder of what lay between him, a man, and me, his lady love. I want this for you, Lucas. And if Miss Tait is that woman for you, then take this ring and give it to her with my blessing."

Emotion clogging his throat, Lucas accepted the ring.

Mama smiled through tears. "Now, there are two things you must know." She held up her forefinger. "Tell Miss Tait the truth. All of it. Leave nothing out."

"And the other?"

A second finger joined the first. "Get on your dukely knees and grovel. It'll be good for you."

"How so?" He wasn't opposed to it, but his mother had more to say.

"Every man from costermonger to King of England must understand the proper hierarchy of a happy household." She paused a beat to give her next words their proper emphasis. "A man's wife is forever in the right. Abide by that understanding, and you'll find joy in your wedded life."

Lucas gave her a swift peck on the cheek, and was out the door in three seconds. He would apologize, proclaim his love, grovel on his hands and knees, whatever it took to make Nell his.

Now that he'd found the perfect woman, he wasn't giving up on them or their future.

RIOTS OF UNEXPRESSED EMOTION CHARGED THROUGH Nell as she strode down the gravel driveway, her gritted teeth keeping the tears at bay.

Only just.

Though her mind had become a tangle of chaos, a single thought came through clear.

If she wasn't very much mistaken, a duke had just told her he loved her and that she was the perfect wife for him and then had proposed marriage in front of his family. A duke, yes, but also...

Lucas.

Lucas had told her he loved her and proposed marriage.

She'd had to leave. What choice had she? Could she trust those words?

Yet... the way he'd spoken them...

They'd hit her heart like the truth.

But how could there be *that* truth when lies lay between them?

All she'd known, sitting at that dining table, was that she needed to get out of those borrowed clothes, out of that duke's castle, and beneath the stars and open air where she could draw proper breath and think clearly.

First, she would get herself back to Matlock Bath. She and Tilly still had three days on their room, and perhaps the Dowager Duchess would arrive tomorrow for her dressmaking session as planned, like nothing of import had transpired tonight. Like Nell hadn't refused the woman's offer of hospitality and rudely marched out of the family castle without so much as a fare-thee-well.

Perhaps... But not very likely. Tonight, she'd most assuredly lost *Galante: Dressmakers Extraordinaire* a valuable client.

Tonight, she'd lost much more, too. She felt it in her gut, in her bones...

In her heart.

She felt it everywhere she could feel.

Loss.

She'd known it before. She touched her locket.

Loss throbbed. It ached. It turned the world dull gray.

But what she knew, holding on to Ewan's locket, was that there was light at the end of that dark tunnel.

And yet these last three days... It was as if a whirlwind had swept her up and transported her into a dream. Past loss had taught her to be wary of such forces, but how had it been possible for her to resist? They'd been a perfect three days. She wouldn't change a thing about them, save one.

Lucas wouldn't be a duke.

He would still be a mister.

But...

Would the last three days have happened if she'd known he was a duke?

The answer was instantaneous and stopped her in her tracks.

No.

He would have told her, and she would have given him the smile. The one that never failed to provide her a safe distance.

She would have only seen a duke. She would've never been able to see Lucas. He would've gone his way and she hers.

Would that have been fair?

No.

For hadn't he known who she was all along? And hadn't he treated her on equal footing to him? Aristocrats were the ones who were supposed to be snobbish. But wasn't she the one with prejudice in this situation?

Was it possible that he'd been in the wrong, but perhaps, so had she?

Then she heard it.

The rapid clip of footsteps crunching across

crushed gravel. She turned and saw a silhouette limned in light from the distant castle racing toward her.

Lucas.

"Nell... Miss Tait... *wait.*"

She almost, reflexively, told him she was Nell to him, but something held her back, even as she allowed her heart to be heard.

It wanted him.

And perhaps this time, with this man, it was safe to follow her heart's lead.

But, first, he had words to speak to her and she to him.

He stopped a few feet shy of her, his chest heaving from his sprint. He stood close enough that she could reach out and take his hand or caress his cheek or press her palm against his heart and feel its steady beat, hard and true, and assure him it was safe with her.

Not yet.

To have the future they could have, the air must be clear between them.

"What is it you have to say?" she asked, as out of breath as he.

"I'm sorry for deceiving you." The apology rushed out in a tumble. "I should have told you my true identity from the start, but—" He shook his head. "No *but.* I should have told you."

It was Nell who wanted to explore that "but." "*But* we were on a holiday. *But* it was to be a three-day lark."

He shook his head. "That's no excuse."

"*But* I would've only seen a duke."

And there it was. The truth. The obstacle. It sat solid in the air between them. The moon and stars gave enough light that she could see his gaze burning into her.

She continued speaking words that needed to be said. "And I wouldn't have seen the man."

98

"I was wrong."

"But you were right," she insisted.

His mouth opened and closed in puzzlement. "Pardon?"

"I would have smiled at you, maybe even have dipped in a curtsy, then bid you a good day and gone on my way. I would've never seen you again, and if I had, I would've kept my eyes lowered and not drawn attention to myself."

Bewilderment creased the space between his eyebrows. "What are you saying exactly?"

"That you were wrong, and..." She swallowed. "I was, too."

Again, he shook his head. "In no way were you in the wrong."

He needed to hear this if he was to ever truly understand her. "In the shop, I cater to aristocrats daily. And many—well, *most*—are rather high in the instep. So, when I know someone is a nob, I paste a smile on my face and make my assumptions about them behind it."

"Likely all correct," he inserted.

"And it's formed something in me that I criticize them for having." She paused. "*Snobbery. I've* been the snob. Not *you*, the duke."

"I'm simply a man." He spread his hands wide. "A man who has met the woman he wants to spend the rest of his life with."

A laugh escaped her. "How like a duke to talk about himself in the third person." The ribbing was gentle and cracked through his seriousness, drawing out a smile that tipped the corner of his mouth. "But wasn't I just your bit of fun?" She needed to know.

"Yes."

She gasped. She hadn't expected that.

"And I hope you'll be my bit of fun for the rest of our lives."

She gasped again, and tears sprang to her eyes.

"I want to marry you," Lucas said.

"Why? There are plenty of women like me in London." She didn't know why she kept offering resistance to everything he said, but she sensed she must. If she was to ever feel secure with him, she must know she stood on solid ground from the start. There must be no doubts lingering between them. "All you have to do is leave Mayfair, or look in your scullery for that matter."

"There is no one else like *you*."

And now they'd arrived at yet another obstacle. "I don't know how to be a duchess," she confessed.

He reached out and took her hand in his large, calloused one. It held warmth and assurance and left no doubt. This duke... this *man*... would be hers if she let him.

"That's the beauty of being a duchess," he said. "However you are is how you're supposed to be. You're the duchess."

And yet one obstacle could remain. "Your family..." She'd sensed how close they were at tonight's meal.

"They like you," he said. "And they already know you."

"As someone they see as a servant." It had to be said.

"They see a talented woman who has made her way in the world with humor and grace. My mother will happily teach you everything you need to know," he added with a smile. "To be able to mold a duchess in her own likeness will bring no small amount of joy into her dowager years."

A chirrup of laughter escaped Nell as tears spilled down her cheeks.

Lucas dropped to his knees.

"What are you on about?" she asked, crying, laughing.

"Miss Elinor Tait," he said, solemn, sincere. "Everything your heart desires, you shall have."

"Come up off your knees," she said, feeling strangely exposed. No man had ever gotten onto his knees for her. She'd never been that special. But, tonight, this man thought she was.

And she understood.

He loved her for who she was, at her essence.

And she loved him for who he was, at his essence.

That was why what they had was true, and ever would be.

It was that simple.

"I only want you," she said.

He shook his head. "A thatched-roof cottage... a tribe of children... soft green grass beneath your bare feet—all of that shall be yours. No one will make false promises to you ever again. Not while I draw breath."

The hand not holding hers dug into a pocket and emerged holding a ring between forefinger and thumb. "Over the course of our life together, I shall give you many jewels, some more ostentatious than you would prefer, but tonight I give you this simple gold band as a promise that what exists between you and me—Nell and Lucas... man and woman—is eternal."

"Oh, what words you speak," fell from her mouth as she felt herself swept up into another whirlwind. She suspected her life with this man would ever feel so.

"Will you be mine?"

"Forever," she whispered, unable to speak properly around the lump in her throat.

He slipped the band onto her fourth finger and tugged her forward. She surrendered into his embrace, her knees giving way as she landed on his thigh. Into the few inches separating their mouths, she said, awestruck, "We've only known each other three days."

He cupped the nape of her neck. "Three days, three

weeks, three months, three years... That's not important. I'd known you not three seconds when I *knew*—" He pressed his palm to her chest. "*Here*." He angled his face and drew in. "I love you, my sweet Nell," he spoke against her mouth.

And there was no hesitation when she said, "I love you, my duke, my man," for the words flowed straight from her heart.

EPILOGUE

TWO YEARS LATER

Lucas rode home from the day's labor, the horse below him in an easy trot, the sky above beginning its transformation from blue to slate purple.

Shearing sheep was hard work, and not for the faint of heart. No glamor to it, but deeply satisfying. And tomorrow he would rise before dawn to do it all again.

The Farmer Duke, indeed.

Ahead, just beyond the dual colonnades of oaks lining the long front drive, a small figure in white appeared, hand held to her forehead, watching him ride in.

Nell.

She'd known he would be returning this way, and she wanted to greet him.

Lucas's heart lifted as it always did when she sought him out after a day's work. Even after a couple of years, their rightness together struck him anew with each passing day. He could see her unreserved smile from here as she waved, their one-year-old baby boy, Charlie, waving from his perch on her hip.

When Lucas had ridden close enough that they

could speak without shouting, Nell asked, "How was your day, husband?"

Hair loose about her shoulders in long waves, and dressed in white muslin adorned with only white embroidery, she was dressed simply for a duchess, but perfectly for Nell, such artlessness only enhancing her understated beauty. She'd rather impressed him over the months as she carved a space that respectfully let everyone—his mother, in particular—know she would be her own sort of duchess.

"A long day," he replied. "There will be bruises."

"Come and sit with us."

It was then he noticed the blanket spread out behind her with a basket to the side. "You didn't cart all this out here yourself?"

She shook her head. "Dockery drove us."

Good. The woman had a lifelong habit of doing everything for herself and had to be taught how to let others help her. It was an ongoing lesson. "So, a sunset picnic?"

"Whyever not?"

"Spoken like a true duchess."

She laughed. "I think your mother despairs of me sometimes."

"She adores you completely." All the family adored Nell, in fact.

She settled Charlie onto his bottom on the blanket and began to unpack all manner of food from the basket—bread, cheese, meats, pies—while he tended Lady Mischief. Though they hadn't told anyone yet, he detected the tell-tale, subtle rounding of her belly in profile. They wouldn't be able to keep their coming addition a secret for much longer.

Charlie, who wasn't yet walking, greeted his papa with a pudgy, slobbery smile before tipping onto hands and knees and crawling across the blanket. "Dadadada," he jabbered all the way, until Lucas swept him up and tossed him into the air, eliciting a round of contagious baby giggles. Impossible not to laugh along with him.

Nell leaned back onto her elbows and watched them, her face lit by a smile. "I'd be careful if I were you. He's already had a pastie."

Lucas made his next toss the last. He wasn't keen to repeat last week's mistake of tossing a baby with a full belly over his head again. He set Charlie down. As the baby crawled away, Lucas leaned over to greet his wife properly with a kiss. Her kiss never failed to light a flame inside him. But now wasn't the time to allow it to become a full conflagration.

He settled back in what could only be characterized as domestic bliss, while Nell poured them each a cup of tea. The sun slipped below a thin ribbon of cloud on its inevitable journey toward the horizon, then suddenly, the slate sky turned dazzling pink. Side by side, silent, they took in the view.

"I received a letter from Tilly today," she said.

"How is her writing coming along?"

"Just legible."

"I'm glad for her." And he meant it. It took some tenacity to learn to read and write as an adult. "What did she have to say?"

"She's in Paris with Lord and Lady Percival."

Lucas chuckled. "Paris doesn't stand a chance."

Nell joined him in a good laugh. "Shall we sleep in the cottage tonight?" she asked.

Lucas nodded. True to his word, he'd seen the old gamekeeper's cottage transformed into her dream thatched-roof cottage. It was now their private retreat.

Nell's head angled to the side, and she froze. "*Lucas,*" she said in a hushed whisper.

Sudden tension coursed through him at the tone of her voice. "What is it?"

"*Charlie.*"

He followed her gaze, and the breath caught in his chest. There was his son, teetering on pudgy legs at the edge of the blanket, burbling his sweet baby coo, attempting to gain his balance as he'd been doing this last fortnight, only this time succeeding.

Then he did it. He took his first step, then another, and another, before plopping onto his bottom. Nell began clapping, and Charlie glanced over his shoulder with a happy, triumphant smile. Nell rushed to him and gathered him in her arms.

When she glanced up at Lucas, tears of happiness shone in her eyes. "His first steps."

And Lucas understood. "On soft green grass."

She nodded, unable to say more.

But she didn't need to, for Lucas felt it, too.

Happiness... gratitude...

For the life they shared together.

For the love they gifted each other, each and every day.

The End

ALSO BY SOFIE DARLING

ABOUT THE AUTHOR

Bestselling and award-winning author Sofie Darling's passion for historical romance began in middle school the moment she cracked open *Wuthering Heights* by Emily Bronte. An instant and enduring love affair was born.

Sofie spent much of her twenties raising two boys and reading every romance she could get her hands on. Once she realized she simply must write the books she loved, she finished her English degree and set pencil to paper. (Ticonderoga #2 is her quill of choice.)

When she's not writing heroes who make her swoon, Sofie enjoys a nice weekend hike, a visit to a crumbling medieval castle whenever she gets the chance, and a slightly codependent relationship with her beagle, Bosco. Visit her website.